"I don't want there to be anger between us, Samantha,"

Thatcher said gruffly as he captured her by the arm, forcing her to stop. "I like the truce we've settled into."

He was continuing to hold on to her. The heat traveling up her arm from his hand, combined with the plea in those dark eyes of his, were making it hard for her to think. Suddenly she found herself wondering what it would feel like to have him kiss her. *He's not interested in kissing you,* she scoffed at herself. "I'm not angry," she managed to say in level tones.

A smile of relief spread over Thatcher's face. "Glad to hear that," he said. Then, as if just realizing that he was still holding on to her, he released her abruptly.

She had the distinct feeling that he was angry with himself for actually touching her....

Dear Reader,

These days, when it feels like winter just *might* last forever, don't forget—you can find all the warmth and magic of springtime anytime in a Silhouette Romance book.

Each month, Silhouette Romance brings you six captivating love stories. Share all the laughter, the tears and the tenderness as our spirited heroines and irresistible heroes discover the wonder and power of love.

This month, meet the dynamic Thatcher Brant, hero of *Haunted Husband*. The handsome widower has vowed he'll never love again. But Samantha Hogan is determined to break the spell of Thatcher's past and win his heart. It all happens in Elizabeth August's SMYTHESHIRE, MASSACHUSETTS, a small New England town with big secrets....

Thatcher is also a FABULOUS FATHER, part of our special series about very special dads.

Then there's *Sally's Beau,* Riley Houston. He's the footloose and fancy-free type, but Sally's out to show Riley there's world enough for this pair of ALL-AMERICAN SWEETHEARTS in Paradise Falls, West Virginia! Don't miss this heartwarming story from Laurie Paige.

Rounding out the month, there's Carla Cassidy's *The Golden Girl,* Gayle Kaye's *Hard Hat and Lace,* Val Whisenand's *Daddy's Back* and Anne Peters's sophisticated *The Pursuit of Happiness.*

In the coming months, we'll be bringing you books by all your favorite authors—Diana Palmer, Annette Broadrick, Suzanne Carey and more!

I hope you enjoy this book, and all the stories to come.

Happy Reading!

Anne Canadeo
Senior Editor

HAUNTED HUSBAND
Elizabeth August

Silhouette
ROMANCE™
Published by Silhouette Books New York
America's Publisher of Contemporary Romance

To Joanne and Rip—a gracious and hospitable
couple (Yes, Rip, gracious and hospitable). Thank
you for terrific meals, enjoyable conversation and
long walks on warm summer days.

SILHOUETTE BOOKS
300 E. 42nd St., New York, N.Y. 10017

HAUNTED HUSBAND

Copyright © 1993 by Elizabeth August

ISBN: 0-373-08922-8

First Silhouette Books printing March 1993

Books by Elizabeth August

Silhouette Romance

Author's Choice #554
Truck Driving Woman #590
Wild Horse Canyon #626
Something So Right #668
The Nesting Instinct #719
Joey's Father #749
Ready-Made Family #771
The Man from Natchez #790
A Small Favor #809
The Cowboy and the Chauffeur #833
Like Father, Like Son #857
The Wife He Wanted #881
*The Virgin Wife #921
*Haunted Husband #922

*Smytheshire, Massachusetts Series

ELIZABETH AUGUST

I've lived in both large cities and small towns. I confess, I loved the small towns best. Every community, large or small, has its eccentrics and its secrets. But I've always felt that in a small town these elements become more focused. They add a touch of spice or, in some cases, discord, that seems to permeate the air and give the town a personality uniquely its own. When the thought occurred to me of creating an outwardly normal, small, conservative, rural community founded on a secret known to only a few but affecting the majority—a secret that in itself could be the basis for eccentricities—I found this too interesting a concept to resist. Thus, Smytheshire and its residents began to take form in my mind.

I have to admit, I've been shocked by how alive the people of Smytheshire have become to me. I've had a lot of fun creating these books. I hope you will enjoy reading them as much as I've enjoyed writing them.

Thatcher Brant on Fatherhood...

Being a parent is a scary proposition. The responsibility is enormous. I know that how I treat my children will affect how they feel about themselves and how they live their lives. I also know I'm not perfect, but I'm going to do my best.

One thing I'm sure about—children need to know they're loved. They have to be hugged and they have to be told they're loved. Children also need discipline. But I want mine to understand that although I may not like something they've done, that doesn't mean I don't like them.

I want my children to grow up to be honest, hardworking individuals. I suppose the best way to do this is to set a good example of myself and hope they will respect me, and because of that respect, accept my values and moral beliefs as theirs.

Tolerance of others is important. Being kind is, too. The Golden Rule—'Do unto others as you would have others do unto you'—has been a guideline for me. It's what I will teach them.

I also hope to instill in them a strong belief in themselves. I want them to be confident enough of who they are and of the values they believe in to be able to stand up for what they know is right. But I also want them to be open-minded enough to listen to what others have to say before they pass final judgment.

I know that, in the end, each will have to walk his or her own path. That's the way it should be. But I want my children to know that I will always be there to help and support them if they should ever need me.

Chapter One

"Thatcher Brant will probably find some way to blame me for this," Samantha Hogan muttered under her breath as she unlocked the door of the large two-story frame house. Like the others on this quiet tree-lined street in Smytheshire, Massachusetts, it was an older home. And like it, the other homes were also two stories high and frame. But each was shaped differently or possessed some other characteristic that made it unique. The one next door, which had belonged to Samantha's grandmother and was now Samantha's home, had a widow's walk atop it. Bright red shutters against the white exterior gave it an eye-catching splash of color. The house Samantha had just unlocked had the distinction of a wide roofed porch that extended around the entire perimeter of the first floor. But unlike Samantha's house, the exterior of this house, including the porch and porch swing, was all painted white, giving the place an air of quiet conservatism. Definitely no red shutters for Chief of Police Thatcher Brant, she mused.

"Da home?" Melissa Brant, the small blond two-year-old Samantha was carrying, smiled hopefully as if she thought her father might be waiting on the other side of the door.

"Not yet, hon," Samantha replied.

The young boy, barely five years of age, standing beside Samantha frowned worriedly. "Is Grandma here?"

Samantha looked down at him. Whereas the little girl was a miniature version of Laura Brant, her deceased mother, Johnny Brant looked just like his father. He had the same dark hair and brown eyes. And he was regarding Samantha with that same dubious expression she was so used to seeing on his father's face. It gave the impression he wasn't entirely certain she was safe to be around.

"No, she's not here, either. It will take the doctor a little while to set her broken leg, then she'll come home," she assured him. Turning to the two-year-old on her arm, she added, "And your father is with her."

Ushering the children inside, Samantha expected to feel like an intruder. There was no doubt in her mind that she was the last person in this town Thatcher Brant wanted in his home. For as long as she could remember, he'd kept his distance from her. They'd had no childhood confrontation that could be considered a basis for a feud between them. They'd just never gotten along. Years ago she'd accepted the fact that there was something in their chemistries that simply didn't mix well.

However, instead of feeling unwelcome, as usual, the interior seemed to greet her comfortably. That was Maude's doing, she knew. Maude was Thatcher's mother, a sweet, kindly widow who, in Samantha's opinion, would add warmth to any home.

Samantha gave each child a big smile of encouragement. Following the death of their mother two years ago, their grandmother had moved in with them to take care of them. Maude Brant was a source of security to them and Samantha knew they had to be feeling anxious at the moment. "How about if we go into the kitchen and see what we can find for you two to have for lunch?" she suggested. "And we'll find something to fix for your grandmother to have for lunch when she gets home."

"Da?" Melissa said again, peering around the foyer and into the living room, clearly hoping Samantha had been wrong about her father's not being there.

"We'll feed him, too," Samantha conceded.

Thatcher Brant glanced at his mother in the rear-view mirror. To accommodate the bulky cast that extended from her toes nearly all the way to the top of her thigh, she was seated sideways in the back of his patrol car with the plaster-encased leg lying along the seat. "You sent the children home with Samantha Hogan?" he demanded in a tone that implied he thought she had lost her senses.

"Samantha is a capable, reliable woman," Maude replied. "And good-hearted. She saved her parents' marriage by coming back to Smytheshire and moving in with her grandmother. Ada couldn't be left on her own, and she refused to go into a nursing home. She was causing a terrible strain on Samantha's parents. And despite the fact that Ada was a difficult woman, Samantha took real good care of her until the day she died.''

"Has it ever occurred to you that Samantha and her grandmother got along so well because Samantha has the same eccentricities as Ada did?" Thatcher queried.

Maude scowled at the back of her son's head. "No. She doesn't fool around with that antique Ouija board of Ada's, and she wouldn't dream of interfering in other people's lives."

Thatcher raised a skeptical eyebrow. "I doubt her sister, Joan, would believe that. As I recall, a while back, Joan, Bob and the kids were supposed to take a trip to visit Bob's parents. Everyone was looking forward to it. Then Samantha consulted the Ouija board and warned Joan not to go on any trips at that particular time. Joan took Samantha's advice and refused to go, and the trip ended up being canceled. Bob, the kids and Bob's parents were furious with Joan. Then a few weeks later, Joan and Samantha decided to consult the Ouija board again, and this time it said the trip would have been perfectly safe for Joan to have taken."

Maude's mouth formed a thoughtful pout. "Samantha says she only got the board out and consulted it about the trip in the first place because Joan begged her to. And she blames you for causing her to give Joan the false warning. She says you had unjustly given her a parking ticket, and that had her upset. It was her distress that the board reflected."

"How was I supposed to know she'd been driving down Main Street and seen Larry Jones take a spill on his bike, so she'd rushed him to Doc's place? All I knew was that she'd pulled her car over on the no-parking side of Main Street." Thatcher's neck reddened as he recalled his embarrassment an hour later when he'd received a call from Dr. James explaining the circumstances and asking to have the ticket torn up.

"You could have given her a chance to explain," Maude pointed out.

"She wasn't around, and I don't have time to wait for people to come back to their cars," he replied.

Maude continued to regard the back of her son's head. "You'd have given almost anyone else a chance to explain. I've never understood why the two of you don't get along. Seems to me you've been at odds since before grade school."

Thatcher scowled. "She's got to be the most obstinate woman in the world. The first day she learned how to walk, she kicked me in the shin just because I was trying to keep her from going out into the street."

"You were barely four when Samantha started walking," Maude countered skeptically.

"That's right and I've been smart enough to steer clear of her ever since," he returned.

"She's not the only one who's obstinate," Maude muttered. Her mouth formed a thoughtful pout. "I've often wondered if she doesn't scare you a little. She's a strong willed woman and you've never liked being challenged."

Looking in the rearview mirror, Thatcher regarded his mother dryly. "You're a constant challenge."

"You have to put up with me, I'm your mother," she shot back.

Thatcher gave his mother an impatient glance, then turned his attention back to his driving. He resented her accusation that Samantha scared him. But, he admitted grudgingly, Samantha Hogan did make him uneasy.

The children had just finished eating when Samantha heard Thatcher's patrol car pull into the drive. The urge to exit by the back door was close to overwhelming. She knew from experience that by the time he entered the front door she could have slipped through the back gate and into her own home. She'd done exactly that on other occasions when she'd been visiting Maude, and Thatcher had come by the house unexpectedly.

A squeal from Melissa jerked her attention back to the children. They'd heard the car, too. Johnny was already on his way to greet his father and grandmother with Melissa close behind.

Thatcher was in the process of getting Maude out of the back seat of the car when Samantha and the children reached the front porch. Maude was a short woman and only a fraction on the plump side, but with the full leg cast, she was cumbersome to manage. "You're not supposed to put any weight on your leg," Thatcher cautioned curtly as she emerged from the car.

"I'm not," Maude replied, balancing on her good leg as she leaned against the vehicle.

At thirty-one, Thatcher wore his uniform well, Samantha admitted. He was a big man, six foot two and weighing, she guessed, about two hundred pounds. The fitted shirt of the tan uniform emphasized his broad shoulders and flat abdomen. Strong as an ox and hard headed as a mule, Samantha thought, watching him slip under his mother's arm on the side of her injured leg and use his body as a human crutch. Half lifting Maude off of the ground, Thatcher carefully propelled her toward the house.

Samantha grabbed Melissa by the hand to keep her from trying to crawl backward down the porch steps. The child let out a squeal of protest and attempted to pull free.

"Melissa, behave," Thatcher ordered. He swung his attention to his son who was partway down the short flight of steps. "Hold the door open," he barked.

Samantha noted that Melissa immediately froze and Johnny scurried to obey his father. *Just as I thought,* she mentally congratulated herself. *He runs his home like a drill sergeant would, and his children are intimidated by him.*

Thatcher barely glanced at her as he passed, making her feel about as welcome as an ant at a picnic. *Well, you knew he wouldn't be glad to see you,* she reminded herself. *And the sooner I leave, the happier I'll be.* She followed Thatcher and Maude inside. As Thatcher guided his mother to the couch in the living room and helped her get seated, Samantha felt Melissa's hold on her hand tighten. Glancing down, she noticed the anxious look in the little girl's eyes as the child's full attention focused on the heavy plaster cast Maude was sporting. "Your grandmother is going to be just fine," she assured her.

Johnny had followed the others inside and now he stood beside his sister.

"Except I'm not going to be able to get around much for the next few weeks," Maude grumbled. A sudden smile played across her face. "Unless I follow Dr. Prescott's advice and go see Celina Warley."

Samantha frowned questioningly. Dr. Reid Prescott had come to town recently to work with Dr. James. Dr. James had been the doctor here in Smytheshire for nearly forty years. Now he was getting ready to retire and was looking for someone to take over his practice. Dr. Prescott was here to see if he was that person. But Reid Prescott was a very practical man and a thoroughly modern doctor. "I can't imagine Dr. Prescott suggesting you go see Celina," she said.

Maude gave a short laugh. "He made the suggestion in a moment of sarcasm. I got the feeling someone had been giving him some trouble. Probably old Paula Bradley. You know what a hypochondriac she is. He probably told her there was nothing wrong with her, then she called him a quack and said she'd go see a real healer."

Samantha knew that a great many of the older townsfolk and some of the younger ones believed Celina had the power to heal. She wasn't so sure Celina, herself, believed it. But she knew from her own experience that once people got a notion in their heads, it was hard to get it out. Then, noticing Maude wince with pain as Thatcher eased the encased leg up onto a chair he'd moved in front of the couch, Samantha pushed Celina Warley out of her mind. "Can I get you anything?" she offered.

Maude breathed a deep sigh. "I wish I'd listened to you when you warned all of us to be careful."

For the first time, Thatcher turned his full attention to Samantha. A cynical expression spread over his features. "I suppose that Ouija board you inherited from your grandmother told you that this was a dangerous day for the residents of our town."

"I do *not* consult Grandma Ada's Ouija board," she replied, regarding him with indignation. "I noticed that the floor of the church fellowship room had been freshly waxed and was a little slippery. And Margaret was leading the aerobics class today. She gets very energetic when she's in charge, and it seemed logical to me that someone might fall."

"You were right," Maude said glumly.

Samantha didn't like admitting that Thatcher intimated her, but his presence was making her uneasy. "How about some lunch?" she suggested, pulling her gaze away from him and focusing on Maude. "When I got out the leftover spaghetti for the children, I saw some roast beef in the refrigerator. I can make you a sandwich."

"That sounds lovely," the older woman agreed. "I am feeling a bit peckish."

Samantha glanced indifferently at Thatcher. "I promised the children we'd feed you, too."

"I'll fix my own sandwich," he replied, his tone making it clear he didn't want her doing anything for him.

He was certainly the most irritating man in Smytheshire, Samantha declared silently. Probably the most irritating man on the continent, maybe the entire world. "Suit yourself," she said over her shoulder, releasing Melissa's hand and heading for the kitchen.

Samantha was standing at the counter slicing the roast when Thatcher entered. "I want to thank you for taking care of the kids," he said stiffly, as he took two plates out of the cabinet and placed them on the table.

"I was glad to help," she replied. She was tempted to add that she didn't understand how his children could be so good-natured with him for a father, but she held her tongue. Glancing over her shoulder, she saw that he had laid out two pieces of bread on each plate and was preparing to spread mayonnaise on them. Telling herself it was only fair to share the work, she cut a few more slices of meat. "Some of those slices are for you," she said as she handed him the plate with the cut meat.

"Thanks," he replied.

For one brief second, he met her gaze. Samantha had always known his eyes were dark, but she'd never noticed they were such a deep brown they looked almost ebony. She'd expected the chill she saw there. What she hadn't expected was the hint of guardedness. Her back stiffened. He and she might never have gotten along, but she was not dangerous to have around. She was a perfectly sane dependable person. Ignoring him, she put the leftover roast back in the refrigerator.

The whistle on the teakettle sounded.

"The mugs are in the cabinet to your right," he said.

She knew he was looking at her again. She could feel his gaze almost as if it were a physical touch. But then he'd always had a disconcerting effect on her. *An unpleasant disconcerting effect,* she qualified. She stopped herself from blurting out that she knew where the mugs were. It wouldn't do for him to know she was familiar with his home. Instead, she simply said, "Thanks." As she took out a mug for Maude, politeness forced her to ask, "Do you want some tea or instant coffee?"

"I'll get myself some milk," he replied.

Again his manner made it clear he didn't want her waiting on him. *And that suits me fine,* she responded silently as she quickly poured hot water over the teabag in Maude's cup. To Samantha, the kitchen seemed to be growing smaller by the moment with the two of them in it. She was beginning to feel claustrophobic. Quickly picking up the plate with Maude's sandwich on it, she escaped.

In the living room, she found Melissa and Johnny studying their grandmother's cast as if they weren't certain what to make of it. Setting the cup of tea and the plate holding the sandwich on an end table, she noticed the lines of strain on Maude's face. "After you eat you should nap," she said gently. "You've had a strenuous morning."

Maude nodded.

Hearing Thatcher's footsteps coming through the hall, Samantha straightened. She had never liked being where she wasn't welcome. "Now that you have your family here to look after you, I'll be going."

"Wait." Maude reached out toward her in a pleading gesture.

"I'm sure Samantha has better things to do than hang around here," Thatcher said, obviously having heard Samantha and wishing to speed her on her way.

Maude tossed him an impatient glare. "You have to go back to work and I can't take care of these children with my leg in this cast. I can't even take care of myself at the moment."

An expression of consternation come over Thatcher's face. "I'm sure there's someone else you can call."

"I'll be happy to make the call for you," Samantha offered quickly, determined to let Thatcher know she wanted to be out of his house as much as he wanted her out of there.

Maude flushed with embarrassment. "I thought Thatcher was the reason you were wanting to leave. If you really have other things to do, then run along. We'll manage."

Samantha felt like a heel. Maude had shown a great deal of kindness to and patience with Grandma Ada. And after Maude had moved into Thatcher's home, she'd always been quick to offer a helping hand whenever Samantha had needed assistance with her grandmother. But there was Thatcher to consider. This was his home and he didn't want her here. Before she could decide what to say, the ringing of the phone interrupted.

Thatcher answered. The frown on his face deepened as he listened. Then he said, "I'll be there as soon as I can. Just try to calm him down."

"You see," Maude said, a hint of panic in her voice as she watched him hang up the phone. "You have to leave."

"I'll stay until we can find someone to come take care of you and the kids," he assured her gruffly.

Samantha felt she had no choice. "I can stay," she said. "I really don't have anything that important to do this afternoon." Firmly, for Thatcher's sake, she added, "I'm sure by dinnertime we'll have found someone who can come and help you out for the next few weeks."

Thatcher looked indecisive.

"Go on, run along," Maude ordered.

Thatcher scowled at the phone; the expression of a man caught between a rock and a hard place on his face. His shoulders straightened indicating he'd made a decision. He turned toward Samantha. "Thanks," he said briskly, then grabbing his sandwich, headed toward the door.

He could have shown a little more gratitude, she thought, frowning at his departing back. Instead, she'd seen anxiety in his eyes, as if he wasn't certain it was safe to leave his family in her care. Mentally she promised him that she wouldn't be there when he returned.

I can't believe I'm still here, Samantha thought frantically as she checked the chicken roasting in the oven.

Maude had napped a lot during the afternoon, thanks to the pain medication the doctor had given her. But even when Maude had been awake, she hadn't been cooperative about finding someone else to come stay with her and the children. She had objected to everyone Samantha had suggested. Either they gossiped too much, or were too quiet, or Maude didn't like their cooking, or she was convinced they didn't really like children, didn't know how to handle children, or they were too old or too young....

The sound of a car pulling into the drive caused Samantha's back muscles to tighten. Thatcher was home. Well, she would leave him to deal with his mother and find someone to help with the house. After a final quick check to make certain everything on the stove was cooking properly and wouldn't burn, she headed for the front door.

Thatcher was standing in the doorway of the foyer closet, putting his gun into a lockbox on the shelf.

"I tried—" She began to explain how she had attempted to find someone to come stay with his mother, but was interrupted by the frantic ringing of the bell she'd given Maude to use to summon her. Worried that either the older woman or one of the children was in danger, she forgot about Thatcher and hurried into the living room.

"I have something to say to you and Thatcher," Maude said with resolve the moment she saw Samantha.

Thatcher had entered behind Samantha. "Where are the children?" he asked, looking around the room.

"They're watching television in the den," Maude replied. "I want to speak to the two of you alone." Her gaze leveled on them. "I want Samantha to stay."

"I don't think..." Samantha began to protest.

"Mother..." Thatcher said at the same time, the tone of his voice letting her know he, too, objected.

Maude held up her hand. "Both of you will listen to me," she ordered. Her gaze came to rest on Thatcher. "Sometimes you get called out at night. That means whoever you hire to come help until I get this cast taken off is going to have to move into this house and be here twenty-four hours a day. Since I'm here a great deal more than you and for the next few weeks will be trapped here, that person cannot be anyone who will get on my nerves. That person also has to be young enough to have the energy to keep up with two children and take care of this house, but mature enough that I can trust her judgment. Furthermore, that person is not only going to have to help with the children, she's going to have to help me, and there aren't too many people I want invading my privacy. Samantha is one of the few acceptable choices. She's also very good with children and she can cook."

Her gaze shifted to Samantha. "Now that Madaline Smythe has married Colin Darnell and they're living in Boston, you're out of a job and can use the income. You put up with Ada and her eccentricities for nearly six years. You can put up with Thatcher for a few weeks."

Her son scowled. "I resent the implication I'm difficult to get along with."

Maude shifted her attention back to him. "Normally you're no more difficult than any man, and I'm willing to put up with your likes and dislikes," she replied. "However, I don't understand this feud you have with Samantha, and I will not condone it. And, I will not let it interfere with my wishes in this matter."

Samantha hated refusing to help Maude, but there was Thatcher to consider. "There is no feud between Thatcher and me," she said, trying to reason with the woman. "We simply get on each other's nerves. And I don't think it's fair for you to force my presence on him in his own home."

"It's my home, too," Maude argued, "at least for the moment. I've rented my farmhouse and leased the surrounding land."

"Mother, you're being obstinate." Thatcher glanced at Samantha. There was a coldness in his eyes that warned her not to contradict him. "Samantha doesn't want to stay."

Maude drew a disgruntled sigh. "Well, there just isn't anyone else I want here."

Samantha regarded the elderly woman worriedly. She'd never known Maude to be so stubborn. "You're probably just having a reaction to the medication Dr. Prescott gave you. It's making you irritable and unreasonably judgmental of others," she said. "After a good night's sleep, I'm sure you'll think of someone you'd rather have stay."

"Maybe," Maude conceded, continuing to regard them both with angry frustration. Her gaze again leveled on Thatcher. "But I want Samantha to stay for tonight. Someone has to be here." She turned to Samantha. "You will stay for tonight, won't you?" she said pleadingly.

Samantha looked at Thatcher. She would not agree to remain in his house unless she had his approval.

"Will you stay until tomorrow?" he asked brusquely.

She knew the request had been difficult for him to make. "Until tomorrow," she said firmly, letting him know she had no intention of remaining longer.

Chapter Two

Samantha awoke to the sound of a child crying. Opening her eyes, she looked around in groggy confusion. This wasn't her room. This wasn't even her house. Then she remembered that she was sleeping in one of the twin beds in Maude's room. Her mind became instantly alert. From the other bed, a few feet away, she heard Maude groan as if trying to fight the drowsiness caused by the painkiller she'd taken. "You sleep," Samantha ordered gently. "I'll go take care of whoever needs help."

A sigh of relief issued from the nearby bed, followed almost immediately by the return of steady relaxed breathing.

Grabbing her robe off the rocking chair as she headed toward the door, Samantha was still finding it hard to believe she was spending the night in Thatcher Brant's home. When she'd gone next door to gather the few personal items she'd need for her short stay here, she'd been tempted not to return. But she couldn't go back on her word to Maude. Ada had not required constant attention, just someone to live with her, make certain she ate properly and got enough sleep. And, Samantha admitted, was kept out of trouble. The last year of Ada's life, during the day when Samantha was working, Maude had periodically checked on her grandmother. Now it was Samantha's turn to repay that kindness.

The crying was quieting into gulping sobs as she hurried down the hall. Then she heard Thatcher's voice. "It's all right, sweetheart," he was saying in gruff loving tones. "You were just having a bad dream."

Samantha told herself to return to her room. Thatcher was taking care of Melissa. But instead, her legs carried her forward to the door of the little girl's room. There she saw Thatcher. Shirtless and shoeless, clearly having taken only the time to pull on a pair of jeans before rushing to his daughter's room, he was pacing the floor with the toddler in his arms and talking to her soothingly. Samantha watched in stunned silence. This was a tender loving Thatcher she had never seen, one she had never honestly believed existed. Admittedly, his wife had often praised Thatcher's fatherly abilities, but Samantha had thought Laura was merely being her usual generous self. Laura saw good in nearly everyone and always tried to think of something kind to say about even the most disagreeable people in town. Naive was what Samantha had always classified her. But everyone had loved Laura. Samantha felt tears warm her eyes. It hadn't seemed fair when the fragile blonde had died so young. But although Laura's heart had been emotionally big enough to encompass the whole world, physically it had been weak. And Melissa's birth had been too great a strain. Laura had died as the child was being born.

In the back of her mind, Samantha had wondered if Thatcher blamed his daughter for the loss of his wife. But watching him at this moment with the child, she could see he felt only love for his little girl.

As if sensing her presence, Thatcher turned. The tenderness on his face vanished. In its place was a coolness, as if he considered her an intruder.

"Looks like you've got the situation well in hand," she said. Turning abruptly, she started back down the hall toward Maude's room.

But as she passed Johnny's room, the door opened. In a voice that sounded as if he was still half-asleep, he said, "Melissa woke me and I'm thirsty."

"Go on back to bed and I'll bring you a drink," Samantha directed.

He'd been rubbing his eyes and hadn't looked to see to whom he'd been talking. Now he stared up at her in surprise. The guarded look she'd seen earlier in his father's eyes was now in his. For a moment, she almost expected him to refuse her aid. But then he nodded and toddled back to bed.

He's treating my presence with the same resignation as his father, she mused as she continued down to the kitchen. There, she found a glass and filled it with water. But when she returned to the boy's room, he'd already gone back to sleep. "The men in this family are clearly more trouble than they're worth," she muttered under her breath. But she couldn't resist smiling down at the young face relaxed in slumber. She knew he was a sweet child. "But he'll probably grow up to be just as arrogant and disagreeable as his father." She sighed regretfully.

She'd left the room and was on her way to the kitchen to return the glass when Thatcher came out of Melissa's room. Samantha's breath locked in her lungs. He was, she was forced to admit, a very virile-looking man. A vee of dark curly hair matted his chest, and the strong musculature of his shoulders and arms that had been covered earlier by the shirt were now visible. Samantha found herself recalling that he had been one of the star football players on their high school team. In fact, he'd gone to college on an athletic scholarship.

"Johnny woke up and was thirsty," she said, feeling the need to explain why she was in the hall. "But he'd fallen back to sleep by the time I got back up here."

"Sorry Melissa woke you," he apologized stiffly. A sudden anxiousness shown in his eyes. "She's been having nightmares lately. Maude says they're normal and I remember Johnny had a few...."

"I'm sure Maude is right," Samantha replied, experiencing an unexpectedly strong desire to reassure him.

Surprise registered on his face as if her comforting words were totally unexpected. Then his expression became shuttered. "I'll take that glass downstairs," he said, reaching for it.

As she handed it to him, his hand brushed hers. A surge of heat shot up her arm. She bit back a startled gasp as her gaze jerked to his face. But he had already retrieved the glass and turned away. Shaken, she watched his retreating form as he moved swiftly down the hall. *Being here has my nerves on edge,* she decided. *But tomorrow I'll be back in my own place and back to normal.* Feeling slightly dizzy, she realized she was holding her breath. Gulping in air, she gave her shoulders a shake. "Go to bed," she ordered herself, and obeyed.

"I can't believe I'm still here," Samantha murmured as she made tuna-fish-salad sandwiches for lunch the next day.

Her mind slipped back to early morning. Maude had awoken in pain. Her leg had swollen inside the cast and was itching unmercifully. Samantha had helped the older woman to the bathroom, then Maude had gone back to bed, taken another pill and gone to sleep.

That had been around five. Samantha, however, hadn't been able to get back to sleep. She'd lain in bed and tossed and turned for a while. Finally she'd gotten up, dressed in jeans and a shirt and gone down to the kitchen. The coffee had just begun to perk when Thatcher groggily staggered in, again wearing only a pair of jeans. Samantha had been certain she would be more in control of her reactions if she ever saw him like that again, but she'd been wrong. A rush of heat, so strong it caused her toes to curl, spread through her.

He'd looked as surprised to see her as she was to see him. "Didn't expect you to be up so early," he said, blinking the sleep out of his eyes.

"Maude woke up a little while ago and needed some help. I couldn't get back to sleep after that," she'd replied. A wayward lock of dark hair was hanging over his forehead and she found herself fighting the most incredible urge to comb it back with her fingers. Using the excuse of finding a coffee cup, she turned away from him. *Something is definitely wrong with me,* she thought frantically. She and Thatcher couldn't be in the same room for five minutes without getting into an argument. It didn't make any sense for her to be having a reaction that felt like attraction!

"Looks like you've already got the coffee started," he'd said, his voice carrying the sharp, critical edge she was so used to.

Obviously he was waking up, she'd mused. Turning toward him, she saw him rake back the lock of hair as he regarded her coolly. The warmth she had experienced a moment earlier became a chill. *This is definitely more normal,* she thought with relief. Immediately she braced herself, certain he was preparing to find something to criticize.

Thatcher's gaze shifted to the coffeepot. "I prefer my coffee strong."

"I always make it strong," she assured him. "But I'll add a little more if you like."

His gaze swung back to her. After a moment of silence, he said in a patronizing tone, "I'm sure it'll be fine. I'm going to go shave." In the next moment he was gone.

Samantha frowned at the spot where he had stood. He was determined to believe she couldn't do anything right. It wouldn't matter if the coffee was perfect, he'd still find a flaw. The urge to put a couple of more scoops into the pot played through her mind. If he wanted strong coffee, she could see that he *got* strong coffee. Then she frowned. The problem with that ploy was that she'd have to drink the coffee, too, and Maude would probably want some when she awoke.

A solution presented itself. Quickly she hurried next door to her own house and got a jar of instant coffee.

When he'd returned to the kitchen a little later, shaved and dressed in his uniform, she nodded toward the jar of instant coffee beside the coffeepot. "If my coffee isn't strong enough, you can add some of that."

He'd acknowledged her suggestion with an answering nod, poured himself a cup and took a sip. "Your coffee will do fine," he admitted.

The grudging edge in his voice had grated on her nerves. It was as if he had wanted her coffee to taste badly. However, she was determined not to allow him to guess that his attitude was having any effect on her. Returning her attention to the bacon frying in the skillet, she said levelly, "Maude said you like bacon and eggs for breakfast."

"I'll get something to eat at the café," he'd replied, heading toward the back door as if he couldn't get away from her fast enough.

She'd started to point out that she already had the bacon frying, but bit back her words. *He really is the most irritating man in all of Smytheshire,* she'd thought as she heard his car driving away....

And now it was lunchtime. She frowned down at the sandwich she'd made for him. "He'll probably want to get something at the café," she muttered to herself.

"Tuna?" a young voice asked in a hopeful tone.

A smile brightened Samantha's face as she looked down into a pair of pale blue eyes. Thatcher might be the most irritating human being in the world, but his daughter was a joy. "Yes, tuna," she replied, grinning at Melissa. "Your grandmother said it was a favorite of yours and your brother's."

"Dad likes it, too," Johnny said, joining his sister.

Samantha was tempted to say that their father would probably find something wrong with the way she made it, but held her tongue.

"What do I like?"

Samantha stiffened at the sound of Thatcher's voice while Melissa issued a gleeful "Da!" and ran toward him.

"We're having tuna sandwiches for lunch," Johnny answered, moving to stand beside his father as Thatcher scooped the little blond girl up into his arms.

Looking at the three of them clustered together, Samantha had the distinct sense of being an outsider—an *unwanted* outsider as far as Thatcher and, perhaps, Johnny were concerned. The boy wasn't as blatantly opposed to her as his father, but he had continued to remain standoffish and guarded toward her.

"I've set the table in here for you and the children," she said. "Maude is in her room. Her leg is still bothering her a great deal, and we decided it might be a little too difficult to move her downstairs today. I'll take her lunch to her and eat up there with her." As she spoke, she picked up the tray containing her lunch and Maude's and started toward the door.

"Samantha." Thatcher spoke her name sharply, bringing her to a halt. When she turned, he said evenly, "I want to thank you for your help."

She knew it was difficult for him to say that, and she couldn't blame him. They'd spent a lifetime of getting on each other's nerves. Down deep inside, she experienced a sting of regret, but she couldn't change the past. "You're welcome," she replied, then hurried out of the room.

* * *

"I suppose the reason you and Thatcher have never gotten along is that the two of you are too much alike," Maude said as she sat propped up on her bed eating her lunch. "You've both got a lot of pride and you're both stubborn as a couple of mules."

"I suppose," Samantha conceded. She'd never really understood the situation between her and Thatcher, either. For as long as she could remember, he'd made her feel uneasy. She didn't like admitting even to herself that anyone could intimidate her just by their mere presence, so she'd fought against the feeling by putting up a front of cool indifference.

"'Course there was the time when you were around sixteen," Maude continued thoughtfully. "I thought you might have mellowed toward him."

Samantha knew exactly what Maude was talking about. She'd labelled it her 'summer of insanity.' It was in the months following Thatcher's first year of college. He was attending a university in the Midwest. Except for quick visits home during the holidays, he'd been away from Smytheshire for the winter. At the time, his paternal grandfather had been alive and this house that was now Thatcher's, had belonged to him. The afternoon of the day Thatcher had come home from college, Samantha had been next door helping Ada with her garden. She'd heard a car pull up and glanced over her shoulder to see him arrive to visit his grandfather. The moment she'd seen him striding down the sidewalk, her heart had given a sort of double beat. It was as if she'd been missing him horribly but just hadn't realized it until he was suddenly there again.

For the next few days, she'd tried denying these new feelings. But they were too strong. Finally she'd given in to them and tried to get Thatcher to notice her. And he had. But not the way she'd wanted. He'd called her 'Kid' and treated her presence with a patronizing indulgence.

Mentally Samantha cringed as she recalled the day she finally challenged him to look at her as a woman. They were shooting hoops on the old asphalt court behind the high school. The action had gravitated into a one-on-one game. He was heading for the hoop and she tried to block him. In the process, she was knocked backward and landed on her seat.

"Are you all right?" he asked worriedly, immediately forgetting about the game and dropping to his knees beside her.

"Only my dignity's been hurt," she replied. He was practically eye level with her and the concern she saw in those brown depths was causing her blood to flow faster.

He grinned, rose and held out his hand toward her. "Come on, Kid, let's finish this match. I only need one more basket to be champ."

A wave of irritation swept through her. She was wishing he would kiss her and he was treating her like one of the guys. Her patience snapped. She accepted his hand and the boost to her feet. Then she stood glaring at him. "I'm not a kid," she said sharply. "I'm a girl. You know, the other half of our species. The half you invite out on dates once in a while."

Thatcher frowned. "You're still a kid to me," he said. Then he shifted uneasily. "And even if you weren't, you're not what I'm looking for in a woman," he added bluntly. "You make me nervous. You're too stubborn and too opinionated."

She flushed scarlet, partly from embarrassment that she'd placed herself in this position and partly from anger because he was being so unyielding in what he wanted in a woman. "Well, I wasn't proposing marriage," she snapped back and stalked off.

All the way home, she kept listening for him to come running up behind her. In her mind she'd pictured him racing up to her, stopping her, telling her that he was wrong and that he did want to date her. But he hadn't.

For the next few days she hung around her house waiting for him to come by and proclaim that he missed her company and that he'd been stupid not to notice her as a woman before. But again he hadn't.

She promised herself that she wouldn't seek him out and she hadn't. But she had started going over to her grandmother's house every day. She hoped that when he came to visit his grandfather, he'd see her and suddenly regret their parting. But it hadn't worked out that way.

She'd been hanging around her grandmother's house for nearly a week before he even came by. Then he was with a college buddy who'd come to town for a visit. She'd been weeding the garden in front of her grandmother's house when he and his friend had driven up.

In a voice that was purposely loud enough to carry to her, she heard the friend ask with obvious male interest, "Who's the cute chick next door?"

"She's just a kid and an obstinate, stubborn one to boot," Thatcher replied curtly and quickly guided his buddy inside.

Samantha had felt about two inches tall. Thatcher Brant wasn't worth another second of her thoughts, she told herself. And that pride of hers that Maude had just mentioned had come into play. From that day on, she'd been determined to consider him as much a nuisance as he considered her.

"I need to talk to Thatcher before he goes back to work," Maude said, cutting into Samantha's thoughts.

"I'll go tell him," she replied, shaking off the memories of the past. They were not her favorites and she preferred to forget them.

Samantha was in the kitchen cleaning the lunch dishes while Melissa sat on the floor taking canned goods out the cabinet, stacking them and then putting them back when Thatcher entered. "Maude is insisting that you stay," he announced grimly.

Samantha turned sharply to face him. "I'll talk her out of it," she promised, determined to assure him she had no intention of forcing herself on him.

"I don't think you can." He drew an impatient breath. "And she does have a few points. We need someone young enough to keep up with the children and take care of this house and her, as well. And if dinner last night was any indication, you're a decent cook."

"Thanks, I guess," she responded dryly, finding it difficult to believe Thatcher was actually considering giving in to Maude's request.

He breathed out heavily. "Sorry, I meant that as a compliment." Agitatedly he raked a hand through his hair. "Anyway, she's also right about her privacy. She should be allowed to have someone she feels comfortable with helping her. So I've promised her I'd offer you a truce if you were willing to stay."

The refusal she'd been so certain was on the tip of her tongue wasn't there. That she honestly wanted to stay startled Samantha. But Maude wasn't being fair to Thatcher. "I know you don't want me here," she said. "I think Maude is asking too much of you. I'll talk to her."

Thatcher frowned. "Maybe your being here would be for the best. There sure wouldn't be any gossip. Of course a few people might start laying book on whether or not we'll kill each other."

It was definitely a backhand invitation, but he was encouraging her to stay! *If you know what's good for you, you'll get out of here as fast as your legs can carry you,* her inner voice warned. Instead, she heard herself saying, "I could use the job, and I do owe Maude a few favors."

Thatcher held out his hand. "Truce?"

"Truce," she replied, accepting the handshake. Immediately she wished she'd avoided the contact, as a surge of heat rushed up her arm.

Releasing her abruptly, Thatcher took a step back and shoved his hands into the pockets of his slacks. "There is one thing I must demand," he said tersely.

That we stay three paces apart at all times, she returned mentally, unable to keep herself from feeling piqued that he couldn't seem to get away from her fast enough. *Considering the reactions I'm having to him, I should be glad he wants to keep his distance,* she chided herself, still experiencing a lingering warmth in her arm. Aloud she said, "And what's that?"

"I don't want that Ouija board of yours brought into this house," he replied, his voice holding no compromise. "You can consult it in your own home in the evenings when I'm here to take care of Maude and the children."

She frowned at him. He was talking as if he believed she hovered over the board constantly, seeking information and advice from it. "I'm not my grandmother. I do not have a need to 'consult' that board."

He raised an eyebrow skeptically. "For your sake, I hope that's true. I wouldn't like to see you gain a reputation like the one your grandmother had." Without waiting for a response, he left.

That there had been genuine concern in his voice surprised her. *It's not really for me. It's concern for his children, who'll be under my influence for the next few weeks,* she reasoned, determined to keep herself from reviving any of those ridiculous notions she'd had about her and Thatcher during her summer of insanity.

A little later that afternoon, while Melissa was taking a nap and Johnny was at a friend's house, Samantha went next door to gather a few more articles of clothing and some other personal items. Standing in the living room, she recalled the grim expression on Thatcher's face when he'd ordered her not to bring Ada's Ouija board into his home. Before Devin Smythe's death, Thatcher had treated anything to do with the paranormal as a joke, a silly dalliance of superstitious people. Now he treated even the mildest show of interest in the supernatural with suspicion and disapproval. Maude had told her about this change in his attitude, but had not offered any explanation.

Only a few people knew the full truth behind Devin's death. The story around town was that he had

been experimenting on himself with drugs he'd de-
rived from his plants. They had unbalanced him.
Madaline, his wife and Samantha's former boss, had
tried to help him but he'd refused to admit he had a
problem. Finally he'd gone completely berserk and
tried to kill his wife. He hadn't succeeded. But in the
attempt, he'd accidentally killed himself. The fact that
his family had sanctioned Madaline's quick exit from
town and her equally quick marriage to Colin Darnell
had given further proof that her marriage to Devin
had not been the happy contented union it had appeared on the surface.

Samantha frowned thoughtfully. She suspected
there was a great deal more that wasn't being told. But
she hadn't pried. It had been obvious that Madaline
had been badly shaken by the experience and didn't
want to talk about it. Following her former employer's instruction, Samantha had closed Madaline's office and arranged for the sale of Madaline's house.
Colin and Madaline had, however, kept the property
Colin owned on the ridge and were having the Kolby
brothers continue with the construction of the house
there. Zebulon Lansky, the old hermit who had sold
Colin the land, was sending Colin regular reports on
their progress.

Her mind returning to Thatcher, Samantha crossed
the room and came to a halt beside a small round table in front of the window. In the center of the table,
perched on a hand-carved wooden stand, was a round
crystal slightly smaller than a softball. "Considering
how our very practical chief of police feels about
Ouija boards, he would never understand about you,"
she addressed the sphere. The sun was dancing on it

and she almost had the impression it was laughing at her. "*I* don't even understand about you."

Her grandmother had told her that this crystal sphere, like the Ouija board, had been in their family for as many generations as anyone could remember. When Samantha was very young, she'd thought that everyone saw the misty images she saw appearing and disappearing within it. Many were cloaked in hooded capes that covered their faces and hung to their ankles. But even when the images wore no cloaks and their faces were in view, their features were vague and indiscernible and she'd had the feeling they were images of people long since dead.

The frown on her face deepened as she recalled the day she had mentioned seeing the images. She had been around nine. Her grandmother had been seated at her Ouija board and Samantha had been staring at the sphere. Thatcher's image had appeared. It was the first time she had ever seen anyone she knew. "What's he doing in there?" she'd demanded curtly.

"What's who doing where?" her grandmother had asked, glancing up from the board.

"Thatcher," she replied. "He's in the crystal."

Ada's eyes rounded in shock. "You can see people in the crystal?"

"Sometimes," Samantha answered. "But I've never seen anyone I knew before. Usually they're sort of misty and dressed in cloaks with hoods that hide their faces. They look like monks."

"What's Thatcher doing?" Ada demanded.

"Glaring at me, as usual," Samantha replied.

"It would be best if you don't mention seeing things in the crystal to anyone but me," Ada cautioned.

Samantha frowned at her grandmother. "Why?"

"Because others don't see things and it might make them nervous to think you do."

This revelation shocked Samantha. Looking hard at her grandmother, she demanded, "Do you see things in the crystal?"

An expression of disappointment came over Ada's face and she shook her head. "No."

Fear spread through Samantha. "Is something wrong with me?"

Ada smiled reassuringly. "Come here," she ordered, and when Samantha obeyed, she gave her a tight hug. "I'm going to tell you a secret that has been passed down through my side of our family for generations. And for now, you must simply take my word that what I am about to tell you has to remain a secret. You must never tell anyone else until you are much older and much wiser and know whom you can trust and whom you cannot. I want your word."

"I promise I won't tell," Samantha replied, still feeling shaken.

"The monklike images you see in the crystal are most likely those of ancient druids. My side of the family has druid blood running in our veins," Ada said. "And it would seem it runs stronger in yours than in most. Your ability to see images in the crystal is a gift, but one most people don't understand. Like our heritage, it must remain a secret. Perhaps it would be best if you did not even tell your parents about the crystal. Not right away, anyway. One day years ago, when your father was kidding me about my Ouija board, I told him about our heritage. The truth only made him think I was a little crazy. And I'm certain he's never mentioned his druid ancestry to your mother. If you tell them about the crystal, they may think I've brainwashed you into seeing the images. They might even forbid you to come visit me."

Samantha had not wanted to keep secrets from her parents, but instinct told her that her grandmother was right. From that day to this, that she saw anything in the sphere had been her and Grandma Ada's secret.

Pushing these memories of her grandmother to the back of her mind, she sighed tersely. "It would be helpful if I knew what the images meant," she muttered. If she did understand them, Devin Smythe might still be alive. She had lied to Madaline Smythe that morning, early in April, when she'd told her employer that she'd been playing with Ada's Ouija board and it had suggested that her employer should be cautious. In truth, her concern had been prompted by an image in the crystal.

Samantha did not spend a great deal of time looking into the sphere. Most of the images she saw there were misty and hooded. And when she wasn't seeing monklike figures, she was seeing Thatcher. But that early April morning, the sun had been hitting the crystal, causing it to glow with an unusual reddish tint. She'd been drawn to it for a closer look. Within, she'd seen Madaline Smythe. Lurking behind her was one of the monklike figures. A chill had swept along Samantha's spine. It was the first time she'd ever seen one of the images she thought of as being from the long-distant past in the crystal at the same time as someone from the present. Because of that she'd felt compelled to warn Madaline.

"But I had no idea what I was warning her about." She scowled down at the crystal. "It's a shame you can't be more explicit."

The center of the crystal became cloudy, and an image began to take form. Samantha drew a disgruntled breath. "Most likely Thatcher glaring at me again," she muttered. But the face was younger. It was that of a boy in his teens with blond hair and brown eyes. She squinted for a closer look. It was Josh Sayer and he had a forlorn expression on his face. "What in the world is he doing in there?" she murmured. Her grandmother had told her that she had a gift, but all she'd ever felt was confused. Shrugging, she turned away and went upstairs to do her packing.

Chapter Three

A look of resolve etched itself into Samantha's features. All evening she'd done her best to stay out of Thatcher's way. She'd fed him and his children dinner at the kitchen table and eaten hers upstairs with Maude. From Maude she'd learned that Thatcher liked to play with the children in the den after dinner. Samantha had gotten her newspaper from next door so as not to disturb his and sequestered herself in the living room. When it was time to get the children ready for bed, she'd offered to help, but when he'd refused her aid, she'd left him on his own.

Again from Maude, she'd learned that after the children were in bed, it was his habit to return to the den to read his paper and watch some television. So she'd sat in the living room working on the crossword puzzle in her paper.

But when Thatcher had come back downstairs after putting the children to bed, he hadn't followed his usual routine. Instead, he'd paced restlessly around the downstairs. Samantha had tried to ignore him, but when he'd walked into the living room, then immediately turned and left, she'd felt like she had the plague. Finally he'd gone out to the porch. That had been half an hour ago.

Samantha rose and moved toward the door. Clearly her being there was not working out. The mildly scented June breeze stirred her hair as she went outside. Thatcher was sitting on the railing bordering the porch, leaning against one of the pillars that supported the roof. She came to a halt in front of him. "I'm sorry my presence in your house is so upsetting to you," she said. "I promise you that by the end of the day tomorrow I'll have convinced Maude to find someone to take my place." Having said what she'd come to say, she turned to leave. But before she had gone two steps, a hand closed around her arm. A searing heat seemed to brand the imprint of the touch on her skin. Startled, she jerked around to discover Thatcher standing behind her.

"Sorry," he apologized, releasing her quickly.

She could tell by his expression that he thought she'd been offended by the contact. *And it's probably best to let him continue to think that,* she decided, still shaken by the reaction she was having to him.

"You don't have to find someone else," he continued grimly. "If your being here makes Maude happy, I can handle it."

Samantha regarded him with an impatient scowl. "It's not fair for me to remain and make you uncomfortable in your own home. I've tried to stay out of your way, but it's clear you can barely tolerate my presence."

He frowned in confusion. "I don't know what gave you that idea. We've hardly seen one another since I got home."

Her scowl deepened. "I'm not blind. It's obvious I'm making you uncomfortable. Instead of relaxing after you put the children to bed, you came downstairs, pace through the rooms, then came out here. It's as clear as glass you find it difficult to be in the same house with me."

Thatcher drew a tired breath. "It's not you that has me feeling so restless. It's Josh Sayer."

Josh Sayer. The name echoed in Samantha's mind as she recalled seeing the teenager's image in the sphere. "Has something happened to him?" she asked.

Thatcher looked grim. "He's gotten himself into some trouble."

Samantha didn't like hearing this. Josh was illegitimate. His mother's family had disowned her when she'd refused to reveal the name of the father, then refused to have an abortion or give her baby up for adoption. Life had been a struggle for Emily Sayer, but she'd worked at cleaning houses and at any other honest labor she could find to support herself and her child. And Samantha was under the impression the woman had done a good job raising her boy. "I've always thought he was a good kid," she said when Thatcher fell silent. She knew she was prying, but she couldn't stop herself.

"He is," Thatcher replied. "And I hate seeing him have a police record, even if it's nothing more than a small juvenile offense."

"Couldn't you work out some sort of off-the-record compensation for whatever he did?" Samantha suggested.

Agitatedly Thatcher rubbed the back of his neck. "That's what I'd like to do. But Malcomb Norwood refuses."

Samantha frowned. Malcomb was one of the three selectmen elected to govern their town. "The Malcomb Norwood who, come election time, claims that all the children of this town are like his own?" she said dryly.

Thatcher nodded. "That's the one."

Samantha had to admit that Malcomb could be stubborn. At sixty-seven, he was solidly set in his ways and had his own entrenched ideas of how things should be done. But he was generally a fair man. That was one of the reasons he'd been elected as a selectman for the past twenty-five years. "Just what has Josh done that has Malcomb so determined to extract his pound of flesh?" This was definitely prying, but she figured that if Thatcher didn't want her to know, he'd simply tell her to mind her own business. Besides, knowing the way gossip spread through their town, whatever the offense, it would be public knowledge by morning.

"Josh picked a few of Malcomb's roses." Thatcher shook his head. "I can't believe the boy would do anything so stupid."

"He picked some of Malcomb's prize roses?" Now Samantha understood. Malcomb treasured his roses. They were his pride and joy. His wife often joked that he cared more about his flowers than he did about her. Actually a lot of people thought that might be the truth—or at least the roses and his wife were equal in his heart.

"That was the phone call I got yesterday. Our selectman had just discovered his roses were missing and he was down at the police station raising hell . . . wanting us to find the culprit and string him up by the thumbs."

"I guess I was so busy with Maude I missed hearing about the roses," Samantha said, surprised this bit of gossip hadn't caused Maude's phone to ring off the hook. But then everyone knew Maude had broken her leg and wasn't in the mood to talk. "But how do you know Josh is responsible?"

Again, Thatcher shook his head. "Seems he's smitten with Amy Buckley. He gave them to her. When her mother heard the news about the roses, she called me immediately. Seems she's not keen on the idea of her daughter and Josh seeing each other."

"She has big plans for Amy," Samantha said, recalling Harriet Buckley's proclaimed desire to see her daughter voted head cheerleader and homecoming queen during the next school year. "I guess a small-town boy with questionable ancestry doesn't suit her."

"Guess not," Thatcher agreed. The frown on his face darkened. "I can hold off bringing Josh in until the end of school tomorrow. But then I'm going to have to arrest him."

Samantha stared at him in disbelief. "For stealing a few roses?"

"For trespassing on private property and willful destruction thereof," he said, reciting the law. "Unless I can change the selectman's mind."

"Or unless I can," Samantha murmured to herself as she climbed the stairs on her way to Maude's room a couple of minutes later.

The next morning, after Thatcher had left for work, the children had been fed and dressed, and Maude was bathed, dressed and propped up comfortably with pillows on her bed, Samantha told Maude she had a few errands to run. "We'll need to call someone to come stay with you and the children while I'm gone," she finished, regarding Maude uncertainly. The stubborn streak Maude had showed when she'd insisted that Samantha was the only acceptable person to move in and look after things had Samantha worried that the woman would not agree to having anyone else there even for only a few minutes.

"I'll call Julia," Maude said immediately.

Samantha breathed a sigh of relief. Maude was back to being her more reasonable self. Julia would be Julia Johnson, she guessed. The woman was near Maude's age and a life-long friend of hers. Julia's husband, Paul, owned the local combination feed-and-grain and hardware store.

"She'll catch me up on all the gossip I've missed while being cooped up here," Maude continued, reaching for the phone on the bedside table. "I feel as if the world is passing me by."

Samantha shook her head. "You've only been inside for a day and a half."

"A lot can happen in that time," Maude replied as she dialed.

A whole lot, Samantha thought. With each passing hour in this house, she was having a more and more difficult time keeping the view of Thatcher as an arrogant insensitive bore firmly planted in her mind. In fact, that picture of him had just about faded completely. *Well, not completely,* she stipulated. He was still arrogant and hardheaded, but he wasn't insensitive. He cared about people. That she couldn't deny.

"I see no blood has been spilled yet," Julia noted with a grin as Samantha opened the door and let her in.

Samantha couldn't fault the woman for her remark. The fact that she and Thatcher weren't the best of friends was common knowledge around town. "Not yet," she replied with a sheepish shrug.

Julia laughed good-naturedly. "Where's Maude and the children?"

"They're upstairs in Maude's room," Samantha replied, glad that Julia wasn't the kind of person who pried. She had no desire to field questions about how she and Thatcher were getting along.

A few minutes later, Samantha was on her way. As she'd hoped, Malcomb was out tending his roses. Parking, she waved to him, then climbed out of her car.

"Couldn't believe it when I heard you'd moved into Brant's home to take care of Maude," he said, meeting her halfway. "Thought you and he couldn't abide each other."

"We've declared a truce for the duration," she replied. Her gaze shifted to his garden. "Heard you had some trouble with your roses."

Malcomb's expression darkened. "Between the aphids and that Sayer boy, I probably won't have a single bud or leaf left by the beginning of July."

"Speaking of the Sayer boy—" Samantha put an edge of uncertainty into her voice "—I was using Ada's Ouija board last night…" She hesitated as if she wasn't sure she should go on.

"Thought you'd packed that board away after that business with Joan," Malcomb said, watching her narrowly.

I'm never going to live that down, Samantha groaned silently. She just hoped that mistake wasn't going to ruin her plan. "Well, I sort of did." She shifted a little to give the impression she was uneasy about being there. "But every once in a while I get an urge to get it out." She regarded him in wide-eyed innocence. "And when I do, I'm very careful about the mood I'm in so that I don't go getting any more wrong messages from it." Her gaze dropped to her feet, as she fervently hoped he would ask about the information the board had supplied.

A silence descended between them for a moment, though it seemed like an hour to Samantha. Then Malcomb said grimly, "Was there something you learned that I should know?"

Mentally Samantha cheered. He'd taken the bait. "The board spelled out Josh's name, then your name, then the phrase *should show leniency and charity.* I asked it what would happen if you didn't, and the planchette went wild and flew off the board."

A look of anger spread over his face. "You saying I should let the Sayer boy off with a slap on the wrist?"

"I'm not saying anything," she replied, keeping her tone totally innocent. "'Course you could get him to do a bit of work around your yard as payment for the roses he took. That arthritis of yours must cause you quite a bit of pain when you have to get down on your knees to weed.''

"How'd you know my arthritis was acting up?'' he asked, the anger on his face fading some. "Ouija board tell you about that, too?''

"You'd be amazed what that board tells me sometimes,'' she hedged. The truth was, she knew about his arthritis because he complained to anyone who would listen. As a result, his aches were common knowledge in Smytheshire. The sound of a car pulling up caught her attention. Glancing over her shoulder, she saw Thatcher. *Time to leave.* "I'd best be on my way,'' she said. "I need to pick up a few groceries, then get back in time to fix lunch for Maude and the kids.'' Waving goodbye to Malcomb, she headed for her car.

"Morning,'' she said to Thatcher as she passed him, but she didn't stop when he paused. Instead, she just kept walking, climbed into her car and drove away.

"I never realized the people in this town thought Thatcher and I were such archenemies,'' she muttered a little later as she drove back toward Thatcher's house. When she'd made a quick stop at the drugstore, Jack Faraday had half jokingly and half seriously asked her if she didn't want to buy a few extra bandages and some iodine. She'd handled his remarks with good humor, but down deep, they'd bothered her. She didn't hate Thatcher; he just made her uncomfortable. The truth was she was beginning to realize there were things to admire about the man.

She scowled at herself. Thatcher, on the other hand, would probably never admit there was anything about her to admire.

As she turned onto Oak Street, the sight of two more cars parked in front of Thatcher's house caused her to breathe an indulgent sigh. She'd figured people would give Maude one day to recuperate, then come calling, and she'd been right. The Mellon sisters' blue Ford was there. The eighty-year-old twins liked to have firsthand information on anything that happened in town. They had both been widowed years earlier. Now they lived together and between them knew every fragment of gossip that had ever passed the lips of anyone in Smytheshire. "And of course my mother's here," Samantha noted with resignation.

"I thought I'd come out and help you carry in the groceries," Sally Hogan said, coming out of the house as Samantha stepped out of the car. Sally was a slightly plump shorter version of her daughter. Like her daughter, her face wasn't beautiful, but it was pleasant. Age had added a few wrinkles, and her hair, which had once been ebony like Samantha's, was now streaked with white. But it was their eyes that were the most outstanding features of both mother and daughter. They were gray.

"Thanks," Samantha replied, waiting for the inevitable.

"If it wasn't Maude who needed your help and if Thatcher Brant wasn't the man living in this house, I'd never approve of your staying the night here," Sally said as she picked up a bag of groceries and accompanied her daughter to the back door.

"You said that when I first told you about Maude's wanting me to stay," Samantha replied.

"Well, I just wanted to repeat it so you would understand why I'm not objecting this time. But I don't want you making a practice of staying in other people's homes when there is a single virile male living there, also. Your reputation is important. You know how people talk, and they never seem to forget," Sally continued in what Samantha classified as her *mother tone.*

"Yes, Mother, I understand, and I don't plan to do anything to hurt my reputation," Samantha promised, managing to get the back door open without dropping her load of groceries.

Setting her bag of groceries on the table, Sally regarded her daughter with concern. "How are you and Thatcher getting along? It's not healthy to live in a hostile atmosphere for long periods of time."

"We've made a truce and it seems to be holding up well," Samantha assured her.

Sally studied her daughter worriedly. "I just don't want you two getting on one another's nerves so badly you end up in a donnybrook and find yourselves in jail for disturbing the peace."

Samantha frowned impatiently. "I don't think our chief of police will throw himself in jail." But the thought that he might like to see her behind bars entered her mind.

"It's not above Mabel Baker to make a citizen's arrest," Sally tossed back, glancing over her shoulder as if she could see through the walls of this house to the house across the street with the turrets and turquoise shutters.

"We will not have any shouting matches," Samantha assured her again.

Sally's mouth formed a thoughtful pout. "I think Maude is trying to patch things up between you and Thatcher. Personally, I don't believe that's possible. I think it has something to do with chemistry—the two of you just naturally irritate each other."

"Well, I'm sure we're both adult enough to keep our truce until Maude's leg is healed," Samantha replied with conviction, thinking that she, Thatcher and Maude seemed to be the only people in town who believed this.

Sally breathed a sigh. "I hope so."

Samantha put the last of the groceries away, then turned toward her mother. "Let's go check on the others," she said, letting Sally know this discussion was ended.

But entering Maude's room a couple of minutes later, she realized she'd only managed to change the location and the people involved in the exchange.

"I can't believe you and Thatcher are managing to survive under the same roof," Pauline Mellon said by way of greeting. Her blue eyes squinted at Samantha as if searching for battle scars.

"We have an agreement. I stay out of his way and he stays out of mine," Samantha returned with a wry smile.

"That would seem to be wise," Rachel Mellon said, nodding her head and making her gray curls bob.

The sound of booted footsteps coming up the stairs caused them all to glance at the door. "I'd like a word in private with Samantha," Thatcher requested coming to an abrupt halt at the entrance to the bedroom.

"Da!" Melissa shrieked happily, deserting the doll she had been playing with and running toward him.

Scooping her up, he gave her a hug as he entered the room. Then handing her over to Julia, he turned to Samantha. "Could I have a word with you in the kitchen?"

She wondered if Malcomb had told him about her claim to have consulted the Ouija board. Even if it had served a good purpose, she guessed Thatcher would not be pleased. But he didn't look angry. He didn't look happy, either. He looked controlled, she decided. Watching him, she admitted that she would have preferred not to have a private word with him in the kitchen. But that would be cowardly and she had her pride. "Certainly," she replied, preceding him out of the room.

"Do you think it's safe to let the two of them go alone?" she heard Pauline Mellon ask worriedly.

"I'm sure they'll be fine," Maude retorted sharply. "After all, they're both adults."

Samantha noticed that this last statement was made loudly enough so that she and Thatcher would be certain to hear it. She started to smile at Maude's attempt to remind her and Thatcher that they should behave, but the muscles in her face felt too stiff to bend. *He's just a man,* she admonished herself, furious that his mere presence made her so tense.

Thatcher said nothing until they had entered the kitchen and the door was closed behind them. Then he turned to her. "I was wondering what you said to Malcomb Norwood this morning. Whatever it was, he's decided not to press charges against the Sayer boy as long as the boy does some yard work for him in payment for the roses."

Samantha didn't want to admit she'd used a ploy that would make her sound as if she was following in her grandmother's eccentric footsteps. "Does it really matter?" she hedged.

Thatcher's gaze narrowed on her with suspicion. "I might want to use whatever you said myself sometime."

"It wouldn't work for you," she assured him. Hoping to make a quick escape, she added, "I really think I should get back to Maude's room before one of the Mellon sisters—or both of them—comes looking for us."

But as she started toward the door, he blocked her exit. "They won't come in here. They're intimidated by me." A look of purpose etched itself into his features. "Now I want to know why whatever you said to Malcomb wouldn't work for me."

She was trapped. Besides, Malcomb was bound to tell someone, and the story would eventually get back to Thatcher. Her shoulders squared. "I told him that the Ouija board suggested he should show leniency and charity."

Thatcher's expression turned black. "I appreciate the help you gave the Sayer boy, but I thought you told me you didn't consult that board."

Samantha stiffened. "I don't. I haven't had it out since that disaster with my sister. The Ouija board was my grandmother's talent, not mine." It occurred to her that if she told him what her talent was he would probably turn purple. She wasn't all that pleased with it herself. "But I did remember that Malcomb was one of the more superstitious people in town. So, I simply rephrased a bit of Biblical teaching. I figured a bit of do-gooding would be helpful to his soul."

Relief spread over Thatcher's features. Then he grinned a crooked grin. "Thanks from me and the Sayer boy."

Samantha's heart caught in midbeat. She'd never seen a man look so deliciously handsome. "You're welcome," she managed, but wasn't certain how she'd put the words together.

Thatcher nodded, returned his tan Stetson to his head and left.

Standing motionless, Samantha watched the door swing closed behind him. She told herself to go back to Maude's room, but instead, she continued to stare at the spot he had so recently vacated. She couldn't be having a resurgence of that teenage crush! she chided herself shakily. That would be pure insanity!

"Are you all right?"

Samantha blinked. The effect Thatcher had on her was so intense his image continued to fill her mind even after he'd gone. Now she saw that her mother had entered the room and was studying her anxiously.

"You look pale," Sally continued worriedly. "I just knew you and Thatcher couldn't get along. I'm going to go have a talk with Maude. Surely there's someone else she can find to come stay with her."

Agreement filled Samantha's mind. But she heard herself saying, "No, don't be silly. We didn't fight. He just said something that surprised me." This wasn't a total lie, she rationalized.

"What did he say?" Sally demanded, not sounding convinced.

"He said thanks," Samantha replied. And it was the shock of hearing him say that word to her that caused this acute reaction to him, she told herself. The next time she saw him, she would feel only indifference.

Sally's expression relaxed. "That's definitely a first."

"And probably a last," Samantha added.

Curiosity entered Sally's eyes. "What was he thanking you for?"

Samantha considered lying. She knew her mother wouldn't be happy with the ploy she'd used. But as she'd already told herself, the story was bound to get out. "I used our selectman's streak of superstition to get him to be lenient with the Sayer boy."

Horror showed on Sally's face. "Oh, I do hope you're not going to start acting like Grandmother Hogan and have the town thinking you've got a loose hinge."

"I have no intention of doing any such thing," Samantha promised.

Chapter Four

A week later Samantha sat at the kitchen table in Thatcher's home, her chin propped up in her hands and a grim expression on her face. "The rest of this town might think I'm perfectly sane, but I'm certain I've got at least one hinge that isn't fastened tight enough," she grumbled to herself.

Her gaze shifted to the clock on the wall. It was two-fourteen in the morning. "I cannot believe I'm sitting here instead of sleeping."

A little over an hour earlier, she'd been awakened by the ringing of the phone. When she'd gotten her eyes open enough to find the receiver and lift it up, she heard Thatcher growling a sleepy hello into it. From the other end of the line she heard Dan Scott, Thatcher's deputy, identify himself. She'd quickly hung up.

But she hadn't gone back to sleep. She'd glanced at the clock. The thought that Dan wouldn't call and wake up Thatcher at that hour of the morning unless it was an emergency played through her mind. Then Thatcher had knocked lightly on Maude's door. In the next moment he'd opened it and peered in.

Samantha had raised up on elbow to let him know she was awake. "Is something wrong?" she asked in a hushed whisper.

"I've got to go take care of business," he'd replied. "Just wanted to let you know I was leaving."

Then he'd gone.

For a few minutes, she'd continued to lie in bed telling herself she should go back to sleep. If she didn't, she'd be exhausted in the morning. But she was too tense. Finally she'd gotten up and gone down to the kitchen and fixed herself some warm milk.

"I can't believe I'm actually drinking this," she muttered, looking down at the cup of white liquid. "What is truly beyond belief is that I'm sitting up waiting for Thatcher Brant to come home." During the past hour, she'd told herself a zillion times that he could take care of himself. Still, there she sat.

She'd spent the past week ordering herself to forget that quirky smile of his. He'd helped by treating her with polite indifference. Still there were moments when she'd catch herself glancing at him and feel a curious curling sensation down deep inside. "Maybe I've even got a couple of loose hinges," she grumbled.

Suddenly she stiffened. He was back; she could hear his car pulling into the drive. The urge to make a dash for her bed was strong. But as she rose, she heard his car door slam. He'd parked up near the back door. He was sure to have seen the light on.

Thatcher glanced around the room as he entered. For a moment, Samantha could have sworn his face had a haunted expression. Then it was gone and he was looking at her. "Is something wrong with one of the children or Maude?"

Samantha forced an nonchalant shrug. "No. I just couldn't get back to sleep, so I came down for some hot milk."

Thatcher's gaze again traveled around the room. "Laura used to wait up for me whenever I was called out at night." Abruptly his gaze came to rest on Samantha once again. "You should be in bed."

She felt like an intruder, someone who had trespassed on a private part of his world, and he was ordering her to get out. Before she could respond, he stalked past her and into the hall. As she heard his footsteps ascending the stairs, she caught a glimpse of her shadowy image in the glass of the kitchen window. Her long black hair was hanging in disarray. The only combing it had gotten was with her fingers when she'd raked it away from her face. Her old terry-cloth robe had seen better days, as had the matching slippers on her feet. "I look like a frump," she muttered.

In her mind an image of Laura Brant formed. The woman had been beautiful, with finely sculptured features. Her naturally blond hair had been long and thick and loosely waved, and she'd worn it tied back from her face with a ribbon or scarf. She'd been as tall as Samantha, around five foot seven, but she'd been much thinner, so thin it seemed a strong wind might blow her away. She had been like a delicate fragile doll, Samantha thought. Although Samantha had a good figure, her medium build pleasantly curvy, she'd felt like a bull in a china shop next to Laura.

Again she glanced down at her robe. Laura would have been dressed in something lacy and feminine, and

Thatcher's eyes would have held a look of invitation when he saw her, not that icy get-lost expression he greeted me with, Samantha thought. A sharp jab of pain shot through her. She gave herself a shake. "I'm not in competition with Laura Brant," she growled under her breath. "I definitely need to get some sleep. Clearly my mind is not functioning properly."

But the next morning as she served Thatcher breakfast, she found herself noticing the angular line of his jaw. There was something extremely masculine about it, and she felt a powerful urge to run her fingers along it. She was so distracted she almost overcooked Maude's eggs.

"I'm just having these peculiar twinges of attraction because of seeing Maude and Howard together," she reasoned aloud later that morning as she sat on the steps of the back porch watching Melissa and Johnny playing. "They make me regret I don't have a special man in my life. Any virile male would have the same effect on me that Thatcher is having."

Breathing a sigh, she recalled the fourth day after Maude's accident. There had been a knock on the door about midmorning. When she'd answered it, she discovered Howard Rutland there.

Howard was a soft-spoken farmer, a couple of years older than Maude, sturdily built and possessing a quiet reserved manner. Samantha had always classified him as the silent dependable type. Like Maude, he'd been widowed for several years. He was also Maude's neighbor and the person to whom she had leased the major portion of her land.

Samantha recalled that before Laura's death Howard and Maude had been spending a great deal of time together. She'd even thought they might become romantically involved. But after Laura's death, all of Maude's time became devoted to Thatcher and the children. She and Howard were still friendly, but they stopped spending time together.

When Samantha had answered his knock on the door, he'd told her he'd come to inform Maude about how he planned to use her land during this year's growing season—what acreage he was planting and what he had fenced off for his goats.

When Maude heard that Howard was there, she'd gotten flustered. She'd insisted on putting on some makeup and one of her newer sweat suits.

Almost as soon as Howard had been shown up to Maude's room, Maude had begun to complain that the walls seemed to be closing in on her. "Been closeted in here too long," she'd said.

Samantha had offered to help Maude down the stairs to the living room, but Howard had insisted on coming to Maude's aid. "Wouldn't want you two ladies taking a tumble and both ending up with broken legs," he'd said.

Watching how gentle he'd been with Thatcher's mother, Samantha had gotten the distinct impression that business was not all Howard had on his mind. "And the fact that he'd been here every day since to help her down those stairs when I could do it perfectly well myself is a big clue that his interest in Maude runs deeper than her land," Samantha concluded.

It was also clear that Maude was pleased with Howard's attention. His visits brought a blush to her cheeks, and she was getting very fussy about her hair and the clothes she chose to wear each day. And whenever Thatcher offered to help her down the stairs, she always managed to come up with some excuse.

Samantha's mouth formed a thoughtful pout. "Looks as if Maude might be getting ready to tie the knot again. And," she admitted glumly, "I'm beginning to worry that I may never find even a first husband for myself." Her gaze shifted to her own house next door, and an emptiness swept through her. She wanted a husband and a family. But the right man had never come along. Thatcher's face suddenly filled her mind. She scowled at herself. *He definitely is not the right man.* A smile played at the corners of her mouth as she visualized how horrified Thatcher would be if he even suspected she'd combined his face and the word *husband* in the same train of thought.

Suddenly the children claimed her full attention. Johnny had been playing with a ball and Melissa had decided she wanted it. When her brother wouldn't give it to her, the two-year-old threw herself on the ground and began screaming and crying.

"Tantrums are not ladylike," Samantha said, approaching the child and squatting beside her.

Melissa paused for a moment to look at Samantha out of the corner of her eye, then resumed her screaming.

Johnny stood watching his sister with a patronizing expression that reminded Samantha of his father. "Here, you can play with it," he said, holding the ball out toward his sister.

Melissa immediately stopped her crying and grinned.

Samantha noted that the little girl didn't even have tears in her eyes. "I really don't think it's a good idea to spoil your sister like that," she said. "You go ahead and play with the ball. Melissa can find something else.''

Melissa had gotten to her feet. "My ball," she insisted, reaching for the toy.

"We can share it," Johnny said, clearly looking for a peaceful solution to both his sister's demand and Samantha's ruling.

"No! Mine!" Melissa shrieked.

"I think you need to spend some time in a time-out chair," Samantha said, falling back on a method her mother had used when Samantha and Joan were small.

Melissa's mouth formed a resolute line. "Ball!"

"You're going to come into the house and sit in the den until you calm down," Samantha said firmly. As she reached down to pick up the child, Melissa let out another angry shriek. Grabbing her doll, she hurled it at Samantha.

"Ouch!" Samantha gasped as the doll's head struck her just below her eye.

Shock registered on Melissa's face and she became instantly silent.

"She didn't mean to do that," Johnny said, quickly coming to his sister's defense.

Samantha saw the look of horror on Melissa's face and knew the little girl hadn't meant to hurt her. Her cheek smarted, but she couldn't entirely blame Melissa. She'd noticed that both Melissa's father and brother tended to spoil her; the child wasn't used to anyone saying no to her. "I think you'd definitely better spend a few minutes in a time-out chair," she said calmly but firmly.

This time Melissa did not raise any objections when Samantha took her hand. She walked quietly beside

Samantha into the house. Johnny followed. Glancing back at him, Samantha saw an anxious expression on his face. Although Thatcher's son had accepted her presence in his home, his attitude was generally the same as his father's—dubious tolerance. Samantha knew the boy was merely reflecting his father's thoughts and she did not hold his reactions to her against him. She'd also accepted the fact that she and Johnny would never actually be friends.

However, she had hoped that she and Melissa would get along. That was beginning to look like a false hope now. Guiding the child toward one of the two over-stuffed chairs in the den, she lifted her into the seat. "I want you to sit here until I tell you that you can get up," she ordered.

Melissa said nothing as she snuggled into a corner like a waif seeking shelter from the cold.

Johnny seated himself on the couch nearby and sat watching his sister with sympathy and concern.

I guess I'll never be a favorite with Thatcher's children, either, Samantha mused as she headed for the kitchen to fix lunch. As a courtesy, she stopped by the living room to ask Howard if he'd like to eat with them. She'd invited him every day for the last several days, but he'd always declined, saying he had to get back to tend his livestock. Still, she felt compelled to ask.

Entering the room, she saw Howard quickly release Maude's hand. "You don't have to worry about me," she said with a grin. "I won't tell Thatcher you two are an item. I'll leave that up to you."

"He was real close to his dad," Howard said, watching Maude anxiously. "Wouldn't want him thinking I was trying to take Joe's place."

"And Thatcher needs me right now," Maude added with resignation.

Sympathy for the couple's dilemma swept through Samantha as she nodded her understanding. "Will you be staying for lunch today?" she asked Howard warmly.

"No. But thanks for the invite," he replied.

Leaving them to say their goodbyes, Samantha went into the kitchen. *It would be nice to have someone look at me the way Howard looks at Maude,* she thought as she began to set the table. Thatcher's image again entered her mind, and she saw him smiling at her the way he'd smiled when he thanked her for helping the Sayer boy. A warmth spread through her. *Any notions you might be having about you and Thatcher are pure fantasy,* she chided herself, forcing the image from her mind and returning her attention to preparing lunch.

But when she heard his footsteps in the hall, she couldn't deny a sudden stirring of excitement. This sensation had been happening to her more and more often when he was around. She'd tried to ignore it, but it refused to go away.

She heard him go into the den. Then she heard him coming toward the kitchen. His footfalls had changed from a relaxed stride to one with purpose.

"What the devil do you think you're doing?" he demanded, barging into the kitchen and coming to an abrupt halt a few feet from her. "You've got my daughter imprisoned in a chair, terrified to leave it without your permission!"

You see, you fool! she mocked herself. *He always jumps to the worst conclusion where you're concerned without ever giving you an opportunity to ex-*

plain. It's pure insanity to think there could ever be any warmth between you and him. She faced him coolly. "She is not imprisoned and she has no reason to be terrified of me. She was throwing a tantrum and I merely ordered her to sit there for a while to calm down."

Thatcher glowered at her in disbelief. "The child is so scared she won't even get out of that chair for me. You must have done something to her."

"No, Samantha just made Melissa sit in the chair."

Samantha could barely believe her ears. Johnny had followed his father into the kitchen and now he was coming to her aid.

Thatcher looked down at his son. "Then why is Melissa so frightened?" he demanded.

Johnny's gaze shifted from his father to Samantha and then to his shoes.

Samantha could see the little boy's struggle. An inbred fairness had caused him to come to her defense, but he wanted to protect his sister, too. Clearly both he and Melissa were worried about their father's reaction when he heard that Melissa had hit Samantha. "I'm sure Melissa and I can settle this between her and me," she said, and saw the gratitude in the boy's eyes.

Thatcher tossed her an angry stay-out-of-this glance, then returned his attention to his son. "What happened here?"

Johnny shuffled his feet, then his little back straightened and he faced his father. "Melissa's scared because she hit Samantha in the face with her doll. But it was an accident and she'll never do it again."

Thatcher's attention swung back to Samantha. Obviously, only just then noticing the difference in her appearance, the grimness in his features intensified. "Is that how you got that bruise below your eye?"

"Like Johnny said, it was an accident." Samantha said, quickly coming to Melissa's defense. "Melissa was throwing a tantrum and didn't realize what she was doing."

Thatcher didn't look placated. "If you think she's sat in the chair long enough, I'd like you to release her so that I can have a talk with her," he requested.

"I'm sure she's learned her lesson," Samantha again defended the child. She couldn't imagine Thatcher actually spanking Melissa, but then she'd never seen him this angry at one of his children. And even if he didn't touch Melissa, she knew that just his disapproval would hurt the toddler tremendously.

"Release her," he ordered.

Samantha glanced at Johnny to find the child watching his father anxiously. Then the boy's gaze swung to her and she read the plea in his eyes. "She's only two," she tried again to defend Melissa.

"Will you please release her?" The impatience in Thatcher's voice had grown stronger.

Bowing to the inevitable, Samantha preceded him out of the kitchen. Entering the den, she saw Melissa huddled even more tightly into the corner of the chair. "You can get down now," she said gently.

As Melissa edged out of her seat, Samantha moved protectively toward the little girl.

"I want you to apologize to Samantha," Thatcher ordered.

Melissa looked up at the woman beside her. "I sorry," she said, tears brimming in her eyes.

Samantha knelt in front of her. "I know and it's all right," she assured her gently.

"You will not hit anyone again," Thatcher continued gruffly.

Remaining close to Samantha, Melissa turned toward him. "Not hit," she promised solemnly.

Thatcher shook his head at her in curt reprimand, then his features relaxed. "Come give me a hug to seal our bargain," he said, kneeling and extending his arms.

Melissa grinned and raced toward him.

Glancing at Johnny, Samantha saw his expression relax. Suddenly he was telling his father about the new game he had invented that morning, and Samantha knew she was forgotten. An unexpected sense of isolation enveloped her, as if she'd been cut from a scene in which she wanted to belong. *Obviously I'm getting desperate to have a family of my own,* she reasoned, and quickly returned to the kitchen.

The soup was heated and she was taking the corn bread out of the oven when Thatcher came into the kitchen. She knew it was him even before she glanced over her shoulder to see who had entered the room. *But then I've always known when Thatcher was around.* The difference was that, instead of the uneasiness she used to experience in his presence, she felt excitement. *My hinges definitely need tightening,* she thought as she set the corn bread on top of the stove.

"I came to apologize," he said gruffly. "I should have given you a chance to tell me what had happened." Approaching her, he gently touched her cheek where a small bruise was forming. "I'm sorry she hurt you."

His fingertips held a heat that caused her breath to lock in her lungs. "It's nothing," she managed, determined not to show the effect he was having on her.

It was difficult enough for her to deal with. She knew he'd be stunned.

Abruptly, as if just realizing he was actually touching her, he jerked his hand away. Taking a step back, he hooked his thumbs in the pockets of his slacks and frowned thoughtfully. "I know I'm overly protective of Melissa and I spoil her."

"I think that's natural," she replied, her heart still racing. "A lot of fathers are that way with their daughters."

A sadness entered his eyes. "It's just that she reminds me so much of Laura."

The mention of his wife caused sanity to return and her pulse rate to slow to normal. "I remember how protective you were of her," she said levelly. She remembered watching Laura and Thatcher together, the way he was always getting something for her or opening doors for her or taking over some yard task she'd begun because he thought it was too strenuous for her. Samantha had told herself he was overbearing, too hovering, and that she would have felt suffocated if she'd been Laura. But she knew Laura had loved it.

A look of angry remorse suddenly came over Thatcher's features. "I wasn't protective enough." Abruptly starting toward the door, he added over his shoulder, "I'll go get the children for lunch."

A lump formed in Samantha's throat. She'd seen the pain in his eyes. The urge to attempt to comfort him was strong. *Laura was lucky to have had Thatcher for her husband,* she thought.

A wave of envy swept through her. Never in a million years would she have thought she'd ever envy Laura Brant. But Thatcher was proving to be a surprise. *Except, of course, where I'm concerned,* she reminded herself. She was sure he would still prefer for her to be out of his house. *And for my own peace of mind, I wish I were.*

Chapter Five

Samantha sat staring at the newspaper in front of her, but her mind wasn't on the printed page. It was on the laughter coming from the den. She wanted to be a part of it.

During the past few days, she'd tried hard to ignore Thatcher. Even more, she'd tried to ignore the growing attraction she was experiencing to him. Neither attempt was proving successful. Since Maude had begun coming downstairs, all of them were eating lunch and dinner together. Thus, twice a day, she was forced to sit at the same table with him. Worse, she found herself strongly affected by his moods. If he was happy, she felt almost lighthearted. If he was concerned or anxious, she had an urge to try to talk to him to see if she could help. Of course she didn't. "I'm the last person he wants butting into his world," she muttered.

"Do you always grumble at your newspaper?"

Samantha glanced up with a start to see Thatcher standing in the doorway of the living room. "Sometimes," she replied, glad her voice had been barely above a whisper so that he could not have known what she said.

"Maude's asking for you," he continued, his voice taking on the polite but businesslike manner he normally used when speaking to her. "I think she wants to get ready for bed."

"Thank you," she replied, her tone matching his as she laid the paper aside and rose.

A few minutes later, as she helped Maude change into a nightgown, she heard Thatcher putting the children to bed. He insisted on taking care of them when he was home. After dinner he bathed them and then played with them until their bedtime.

"I know spending time with his children is important, but my son needs to take some time for himself," Maude said, frowning at her closed door. Her gaze shifted to Samantha. "Did you know he hasn't dated anyone since Laura died? He's a young man. He needs to get on with his life."

The thought that she would like Thatcher to devote some time to *her* entered Samantha's mind. *You're being idiotic,* she chided herself. She and Thatcher probably couldn't be alone for more than five minutes without finding something to argue about. "He seems perfectly happy with his life as it is," she said.

Maude's frown deepened. "It's as if, where marriageable women are concerned, he's put a lock on his heart and refuses to let in any woman other than Laura. He shouldn't shut himself away like that. It's not right."

"I'm sure he'll start dating again when he's ready." Samanatha recalled the sadness she'd seen in his eyes a few days earlier when he'd spoken of Laura. "He was very much in love with his wife," she added, again thinking that Laura had been a very lucky woman.

"He did adore her," Maude conceded. An anxious tone entered her voice. "She wasn't perfect, but he's made her memory into something so sterling that no other woman will ever be able to compete with it."

"Maybe he's one of those people who only have one great love in their life and never find another." It occurred to Samantha that she was saying this as much for herself as for Maude.

Maude sighed in resignation. "I suppose you could be right. And he does have a nice little family."

A very nice family, Samantha agreed on her way downstairs a little while later. Again the urge to be a part of his family came over her. "This is crazy!" she scolded herself under her breath.

Her jaw firmed. She had to do something to get this notion out of her head. Avoiding being alone with him hadn't helped. *Maybe I should spend some time with him instead,* she reasoned. *No doubt we'll fight, and that will end these ridiculous fantasies.*

Thatcher was on the porch. Stepping out into the night, Samantha drew a deep breath of the softly fragrant air. "Clearly summer is my season for craziness," she mused. She saw him sitting on the rail, leaning against one of the roof pillars. He turned to her, and a warmth spread through her. *This has got to stop!* she ordered herself. "Nice evening," she said, coming to within about five feet of him, then stopping. *This is close enough,* she cautioned herself, fighting the urge to move closer.

He straightened a little and his manner was coolly businesslike as he asked, "Is there a problem you need to talk to me about?"

Considering how determinedly she'd avoided being alone with him, she couldn't fault him for thinking she'd seek him out only if she had a problem to discuss with him. "No." Her legs were feeling slightly weak. *You're acting like a schoolgirl trying to talk to the object of her first crush,* she chided herself. *Be nonchalant!* Moving to the rail near the next pillar, she seated herself and leaned against that pillar facing him. About four feet separated them. "Just thought I'd come outside for a while. It's such a nice night."

"Yes, it is."

He was watching her guardedly as if he didn't quite trust her. "Nice and peaceful," she added.

"Looks that way," he replied.

Causal conversation has never been one of my strong points, she thought frantically, trying to think of something original to say. She'd been avoiding looking directly at him, hoping that would allow her to think more clearly. Now she glanced at him. His gaze had shifted from her to the street, and there was a grim set to the line of his jaw. She recalled he had seemed withdrawn at dinner, as if he had something on his mind. "You look worried," she heard herself saying. His gaze swung to her. There was a coldness in his eyes. She'd meant to make casual conversation. She knew he wouldn't like her prying into anything he considered his business. But then, maybe if he told her to go away and leave him alone it would help her get over these ridiculous reactions she was having to him.

For a long moment, he regarded her in terse silence, then he drew a harsh breath. "Got a call today. Luther Conley is out of prison."

Samantha pictured Luther. He was medium in build, about five ten, with brown hair and blue eyes. He had a boyishly handsome face and the ability to charm the fuzz off of a peach. Mary, his wife, was a native of Smytheshire. She was a petite brunette, a little on the homely side and four years younger than Samantha. When the newlyweds had moved to town, everyone had been amazed that Mary had made such a good catch. What no one realized was that beneath his kind fun-loving exterior, Luther had a real mean streak. Behind closed doors, he'd beaten his wife.

Because Mary was embarrassed, frightened or still in love—Samantha had never been sure of her motives—Mary had lied and told people she was clumsy. Then one night Luther had gotten so angry he'd lost all control and beaten Mary to within an inch of her life. The neighbors had heard her screams and called Thatcher. When he'd arrived, he'd found Mary unconscious, bleeding and bruised, with a concussion, a broken arm and a broken leg. It had been a couple of days before the doctors were even sure she was going to live.

Unwilling to face Luther's brutality any longer, Mary had filed charges and testified against him. He'd been convicted and sent to prison. But before he'd been taken away, he'd asked to speak to Mary. People had thought he wanted to apologize to her for the pain he'd inflicted upon her. Instead, he'd promised her that she would regret having turned against him.

"Have you warned Mary?" she asked, fearful for the other woman.

"I've warned her and put out the word that I want to know if anyone sees Luther in town," he replied.

Samantha was studying him. He'd always done his job well. Before she'd moved in here, she'd convinced herself that to him that was all his police work was— a job. Now, after having seen how he'd worried about the Sayer boy and was worried about Mary, she knew she'd been wrong. He cared a great deal about the citizens of this town. "Maybe Mary should consider staying with relatives out of town for a few weeks."

Agitatedly Thatcher raked a hand through his hair. "I suggested that to her. But she pointed out that I couldn't even be sure Luther would come back here. She's gotten a divorce from him, found herself a job down at Johnson's Hardware and Feed and Grain Store, and she and my deputy are getting to be a real item. She says she's rebuilt her life and she refuses to let Luther rob her of it."

Samantha couldn't stop an admiring smile. "Mary turned out to have a tougher core than any of us thought. She's learned to stand solidly on her own two feet."

The worry on Thatcher's face deepened. "I still don't want to see her have to square off with Luther. I told her to call me if she hears from him."

"He might not come back here," Samantha said encouragingly. "This isn't his hometown and he never liked it here. Besides, he always struck me as being a bully. Maybe he'll decide to leave well enough alone and stay away."

"I hope so." Thatcher suddenly looked self-conscious. "Sorry. You came out here to relax and enjoy the evening, and I've been depressing you with talk about my work."

"I don't mind. You're more informative than the newspaper," she replied, wishing there was some way she could ease the lines of stress on his face. *This isn't working,* her inner voice screamed at her. Instead of finding his company boring, she was glad she was there with him.

He smiled a tired smile. "Thanks. I know talking about Luther won't solve the problem, but it helps."

Samantha's heart began to pound faster. He was actually admitting that talking to her had been a help to him. *No, he admitted to having been helped by having someone to talk to,* she corrected herself. *Anyone with a sympathetic attitude would have sufficed.* Determined to keep her thoughts in the proper perspective, she said, "I guess you miss having Laura to talk to."

His features suddenly hardened back into grim lines. "I never discussed my work with Laura. She didn't like to hear about the bad that was in people. Besides, it caused her to worry about me, and I didn't want that." Abruptly he rose. "Got a few things I need to take care of before I go to bed," he said.

Before Samantha could utter a quick good-night, he'd strode inside. "You sure know how to get rid of him fast," she muttered. She told herself she should be relieved. Instead she felt deserted.

Maybe avoiding him would be for the best, she concluded as she gazed at the moon.

The next evening she was again trying to read the newspaper and to ignore the sounds of the children playing mingled with Thatcher's laughter when she noticed that they'd fallen silent. Hearing footsteps in the hall, she peered around her newspaper just as Thatcher entered the living room.

"Johnny wants me to play a game with him," he said, coming to a halt just inside the doorway. "I was wondering if you'd mind coming in and keeping Melissa occupied for a little while?" He shifted uneasily. "You deserve a break from them after taking care of them all day, so if you don't want to, just say so."

He was inviting her to join them—out of necessity, she quickly forced herself to note. And it was obvious he was uncomfortable making this offer. The thought that it would be smart to refuse flashed through her mind. But she couldn't resist accepting. "I don't mind playing with Melissa," she replied, telling herself this was part of the job they'd hired her to do.

In the den, Melissa greeted her happily. Still, it wasn't easy to keep the little girl distracted from the cards her father and brother were playing with, but Samantha managed. Actually she didn't mind the challenge. It helped keep her attention off Thatcher. Admittedly she was constantly aware of him stretched out on the floor with the cards spread out between him and his son. And once when Melissa was occupied with one of her dolls, Samantha couldn't stop her gaze from traveling along the muscular length of his legs to his strong back and broad shoulders. A shiver of delight raced along her spine. Immediately she returned her attention to Melissa. But in the background she heard Thatcher's voice, his tone gentle and loving and full of fun. She drew a shaky breath. There was a warmth in this room, a soothing, comforting, deliciously intoxicating warmth, and again she found herself wanting to be a permanent part of this family.

"Bedtime," Thatcher announced as he and Johnny finished their game.

Samantha glanced over to see the boy beaming and knew he'd won. "One more game," he was requesting and Samantha found herself wanting Thatcher to grant this wish. She told herself it was for the boy's sake, but deep inside she knew it was because she didn't want being in here with Thatcher and his children to end. *Foolish* woman, she chided herself.

"You've beaten me soundly twice," Thatcher pointed out, mussing the boy's hair playfully. "Tomorrow night, we'll play again."

"Me play, too," Melissa said running to her father and grabbing him around the neck.

"We'll see," Thatcher replied, shifting himself into a sitting position and giving her a hug. Then, continuing to hold her, he rose to his feet. Reaching down, he lifted Johnny up and tossed him over his free shoulder. The boy giggled as Thatcher carried him and his sister out of the room.

Left by herself, Samantha's gaze traveled around the room. It was just a room now, with no special feel. An intense lonliness enveloped her. The three of them had left her behind as if she were nothing more than a toy or a stick of furniture. *Well, you knew you weren't really a part of their little group,* she admonished herself for this sudden bout of self-pity. She'd never been one to indulge in wasteful emotions. Shaking off the uncomfortable sensation, she began to straighten the room.

"The kids wanted to say good-night."

Samantha jerked around to see Thatcher returning with the children. He set them on the floor and they both rushed over to give her a hug, then quickly raced back to their father. He scooped them up and in the next moment, they were gone.

Samantha felt her facial muscles forming a smile. *They were only being polite,* she told herself. Still, the feel of the little arms around her had brought the warmth back to this room, and this time it lingered.

After putting the den in order, she started back to the living room and her newspaper. But she was feeling too restless to sequester herself inside four walls. Changing direction, she wandered out onto the porch. There was a sweetness in the air. Seating herself on the rail and leaning against a pillar, she looked up at the half-moon. "A night for lovers," she murmured under her breath. Thatcher's image entered her mind. "Or a night for insanity," she added.

"I want to thank you for playing with Melissa."

Her body tensed as Thatcher joined her on the porch. "I enjoyed playing with her," she replied. Then, trying to keep her position in his home in the proper perspective, she said for her own sake, "Besides, that's my job."

Taking a seat on the rail next to the pillar he regarded her with a shuttered expression. "When Maude insisted on hiring you, I wasn't so sure she was making the right choice. But you're very good with Melissa and Johnny."

She smiled wryly. This was the Thatcher she knew— the one who always underestimated her abilities. "You sound surprised."

"Maybe a little," he returned uncomfortably. "I've always thought you didn't particularly enjoy being around children."

He made her sound coldhearted, and that hurt. "I like children," she declared. "I'd like to have a couple of my own someday."

"You'd make a good mother."

Samantha blinked, barely able to believe he'd actually said that. And the tone of his voice let her know he'd meant it. "Thanks," she managed, then heard herself adding, "But first I need to find a husband. I'm old fashioned that way."

He studied her thoughtfully. "A lot of people, including me, thought that you and Alan Blaine might get married."

"I thought so, too," she admitted, recalling the blue-eyed high school history teacher. "Then one day I was at his home for a big family gathering. I like his family and I like him, but suddenly I felt totally out of place. It wasn't anything anyone said or did. I just found myself wanting to be anywhere but there." Samantha stopped, shocked by how open she'd been. But Thatcher was easy to talk to. Another wave of shock swept through her. Never in a million years would she have thought she'd think of anything about him as being easy. She'd always considered him hard, cold and insensitive. "Anyway, I know I made the right decision," she finished, too tense to allow a silence to descend between them. "Alan and Joyce have been married for three years now and seem happy together."

Thatcher nodded. "I always thought he was a little too mild-mannered for you, anyway."

Samantha's back stiffened. *Fool!* she chided herself. She'd been behaving as if she was talking to a friend. But Thatcher wasn't her friend. He'd always been critical of her, and she'd let down her guard and given him the opportunity to take a fresh jab at her. "I'm not as difficult to get along with as you seem to think I am."

"I didn't mean that the way it sounded," he said with gruff apology. "I just meant that you seem like a woman who would need a man who was stronger-willed, who would be a more even match."

Samantha's jaw tensed in anger. "You make me sound like a shrew."

Thatcher raked a hand through his hair. "I didn't mean to do that, either." He grimaced. "I seem to be shoving my foot farther into my mouth every time I open it."

Unexpectedly Samantha experienced a stirring deep inside. He looked so boyishly handsome as he tried to squirm out of this corner he'd worked himself into. *Thoughts like that are only going to cause trouble,* she warned herself. "Maybe we should forget this conversation ever happened and say good-night?" she suggested.

"Maybe we should," he agreed.

But as she rose and moved toward the door, he suddenly got up and captured her by the arm, forcing her to stop. "I don't want there to be anger between us, Samantha," he said as she turned toward him. "I like the truce we've settled into."

He continued to hold on to her. The heat traveling up her arm from his hand combined with the plea in his dark eyes were making it hard for her to think. Suddenly she found herself wondering what it would feel like to have him kiss her. *He's not interested in kissing you,* she scoffed at herself. Suddenly afraid he might read these unsettling reactions in her face, she grew desperate to escape. "I'm not angry," she managed to say in level tones. She forced a smile. "We still have our truce."

Smiling in return, he said with a note of relief, "Glad to hear that." As if just then realizing he was still holding on to her, he released her abruptly. "Sorry," he apologized.

She had the distinct feeling he was angry with himself for actually touching her. She felt like telling him that she was perfectly safe to be around. But she had just assured him that they indeed had a truce and she was determined to keep her word. "No harm done," she said coolly, as if she'd barely noticed the contact between them. "Good night."

But a little later as she lay in her bed, she recalled the heat of his touch. It didn't seem possible, but she could still feel a lingering warmth where his hand had rested on her arm. Even more, she remembered looking up into those dark eyes of his. Her whole body tensed as she again wondered what it would have felt like if he'd kissed her. *He would probably have been so appalled he would have gone in and gargled antiseptic,* she told herself, furious that her mind was traveling along such a ludicrous path. *I think it's time I began seriously looking for a husband,* she decided. Thatcher's image grew stronger. Frustration filled her. *Be realistic!* she scolded herself. He wasn't interested in her, nor would he ever be.

Chapter Six

The thought that she'd been living in Thatcher's home for nearly three weeks played through Samantha's mind. It was lunch time. As she sat at the table eating with Thatcher, the children and Maude, she tried not to think about how comfortable she felt among them. She'd been hoping she'd experience that same I-don't-belong-here realization she'd had at Alan's home. Instead, with each passing day, she felt closer to the children and Maude—and more drawn toward Thatcher.

At the moment, she was covertly studying his right hand, which was wrapped around his coffee cup. It was strong—she knew that from when he'd caught her arm. His hold had been loose but she'd still felt the strength. It was a very masculine hand, large with squarish fingers. There was a small scar on the thumb.

Her gaze shifted to his left hand as it reached out to ruffle Johnny's hair. There was a large scar across the back of it. She knew he'd gotten that trying to subdue a drunk with a knife. Her stomach knotted at the thought of the pain he must have felt. She jerked her attention back to her food. *You've got to stop thinking about him so much,* she ordered herself.

The ringing of the doorbell interrupted the story Johnny was telling. "I'll get it," Samantha said quickly, glad of any excuse to get away from Thatcher for a few minutes and force her mind back onto a more rational path.

Reaching the front door, she discovered Olivia Stuart standing there. Olivia and her husband, Bruce, were both in their late eighties. Bruce didn't get around very well any more, but Olivia was still spry for her age. "I want to see Thatcher," Olivia demanded the moment she saw Samantha.

Samantha's legs weakened. The elderly woman was bobbing her head in an agitated fashion as she spoke, and it was clear she was upset. Everyone in town had been keeping an eye out for Luther Conley. Samantha had been hoping the man wouldn't return. If he did, it was certain to mean trouble. Although she kept telling herself that Thatcher could take care of himself, she was afraid for him. "He's in the kitchen," she said, stepping aside to allow Olivia to precede her. Unable to control her concern, she asked, "Have you seen Luther?"

"Ain't seen him but if I had, I'd have gone home and gotten Bruce's rifle and run that rabble out of town myself," she retorted, continuing toward the kitchen without a backward glance.

Watching Olivia's frail body move with its slightly awkward gait, caused by arthritic knees and ankles, Samantha admired the woman's spunk. She also couldn't help wondering who or what had brought the woman here.

Thatcher looked surprised, then guarded as Olivia entered the kitchen. He rose as she came around the table toward him.

Reaching him, Olivia stiffened her back until she was standing as straight as her arthritis would allow. Then she held out her hands and said, "I drove myself here. You can put the cuffs on me and take me to jail, but I intend to keep on driving anywhere in this town I want to go." Defiance glistened in her eyes. "Go ahead. Slap the cuffs on. I want your children to see what kind of man you are, harassing old women."

"I am not going to put handcuffs on you or take you to jail," Thatcher said. "But you *are* going to have to stop driving. You didn't pass the eye test."

"It's a conspiracy to get us older people off the roads," she seethed. Her gaze swung to Maude. "They got a new eye chart in."

"Because you had the old one memorized," Thatcher pointed out.

Olivia tossed him a furious glance, then swung her attention to Samantha. "You've been right about this man all along. He's—" her face contorted into a look of rage as she fought to find words "—he's high-handed, imperious and tyrannical."

Samantha glanced at Thatcher. He showed no anger at the insults being thrown at him. She admired him for his tolerance. She knew it couldn't be easy to stand there and take those insults calmly, especially in front of his children. "Since I've been here taking care of Maude and the children," she said to Olivia, "I've revised my opinion of him. I'm sure he didn't mean to upset you. He's just doing his job."

Rewarding Samantha with a harrumph, Olivia swung her attention to Maude. "He's your son. Thought you'd have raised him to respect his elders."

"He does," Maude answered angrily.

Samantha heard a small sob and saw tears begin to run down Melissa's cheeks. Quickly she lifted the child into her arms and glanced at Johnny to see if this scene was troubling him, too. But the boy was simply watching with interest.

Olivia now looked totally distraught. "I didn't mean to upset the child," she said with remorse.

Somewhat placated by Samantha's protective embrace, Melissa stopped sobbing. But she kept her arms around Samantha's neck, watching Olivia out of the corner of her eye.

"You're going to have to face the fact you're getting old, Olivia. Your eyesight isn't what it used to be and neither are your reflexes," Maude said sternly. "You don't want to cause an accident or hurt anyone, do you?"

Tears brimmed in the elderly woman's eyes. Then her shoulders straightened with pride. "I've never done anyone any harm and don't ever want to. But Bruce can't drive anymore, and now with my license taken away from me, we've got no way to get around."

"I'm sure your daughter or son or anyone of that bevy of grandchildren and great-grandchildren you have will be happy to give you a lift when you need one," Maude said. "And when I get this leg out of its cast, I'll be happy to help."

Olivia's jaw firmed and her back straightened even more. "I appreciate the offer, but you have your own family to see to. And my children and grandchildren have their own lives to live. I refuse to go begging anyone to chauffeur us. I've stood on my own two feet all my life. Ain't never asked nothing of nobody, and I won't start now.''

"You could offer to pay those two great-grandsons of yours to drive you around," Thatcher suggested. "I'm sure they could use the money."

Olivia's gaze swung to him, anger again spreading over her face as if she was furious with him for even speaking. She opened her mouth to respond, then suddenly clamped it shut. For a moment she regarded him in silence, then her angry expression was replaced with one of relief. "They could," she admitted. She drew a steadying breath as embarrassment added a pink tint to her cheeks. "Guess I sort of overreacted. But it's not easy having some of my freedom taken away."

"No one likes to have any of their freedom taken away," Thatcher replied sympathetically.

Olivia turned her attention to Melissa. "She's just like her mother—hates to see anyone unhappy or distressed." Moving near, she touched Melissa lightly on the cheek. "Such a gentle soul. Guess Laura didn't marry so badly, after all."

Samantha saw the shadow of pain in Thatcher's eyes, then they became shuttered. *No, Laura didn't marry badly at all,* she thought.

Melissa wiggled to be free and Samantha put her down. Immediately the child ran to her father. He scooped her up in his arms and hugged her reassuringly.

The tenderness on his face tugged at Samantha's heart. Suddenly she felt like an intruder in Laura's house. A shaft of pain pierced her. *I want to belong here,* she admitted. *But that would never happen. This was Laura's house and it would always be hers and no one else's.* "I'll give you a ride home," she said to Olivia. "You can send someone for your car later."

"I can walk," Olivia protested. "You finish your lunch."

"I insist." Samantha was already moving toward the kitchen door.

"Well, it *is* a mile." Olivia looked down at her legs and arthritic ankles. "I could make it, but it'd take a while and I don't like leaving Bruce alone for too long."

Samantha smiled and offered the woman her arm for support. Olivia accepted and the two left the house.

"Too bad you and Thatcher have never been able to get along," Olivia said as Samantha drove her home. "He'd make a good husband, and he's got a nice little family there." Her gaze leveled on Samantha. "You're not getting any younger. I know your mother would like to see you married."

During the past few years, Samantha had gotten used to remarks like this. It seemed that, at least in this town, once a woman got past the age of twenty-five and still wasn't married, people began to worry she might end up a spinster. And, maybe in her case, she admitted, they were right. But she wasn't about to settle for just any man. "I'm sure I'll find my Mr. Right some day," she replied noncommittally. Again Thatcher's image came into her mind. *He wouldn't even want to be on my list of possibilities,* she reminded herself, and shoved the image out.

An expression of reprimand came over Olivia's features. "Heard you went to see Malcomb with a message from that Ouija board Ada willed you. Hope you aren't going to get squirrelly like your grandmother.''

"No, I'm not going to start behaving like my grandmother,'' Samantha assured her.

Olivia shook her head. "It's a shame about you and Thatcher,'' she said, returning to her previous topic of discussion. '' 'Course you're as different from Laura as night from day. If he were to marry again, guess he'd want someone more like her.''

He'd want a clone, Samantha thought.

A few minutes later as she walked Olivia to her door, the old woman lowered her voice and leaned toward Samantha. "Of course, if you were to get out that Ouija board and it gave you a message for me or Bruce, I'd be grateful if you'd call.''

Samantha caught herself before she blurted that she'd put the board away after the incident with her sister and had no intention of ever using it again. That bit of information was sure to get back to Malcomb and he would be furious with her for having lied about getting a message for him. "I will,'' she promised.

Driving back to Thatcher's place, a feeling close to desperation began to invade Samantha. A solution presented itself. It wasn't a particularly rational solution, she admitted but she was willing to try anything to get her mind back on a more normal path.

Later that afternoon, while Melissa was taking her nap and Johnny was playing checkers with Howard, Samantha made an excuse about needing something from her house. All the way across the lawn, she called herself an idiot. "I really can't believe you would even consider this,'' she admonished her reflection in the hall mirror on her way to the living room.

Still, she kept going until she reached the table in front of the window that held the antique crystal ball. She'd never tried to direct her thoughts when looking into the ball. She'd simply accepted whatever it wanted to show her.

She drew a deep breath. The truth was that it scared her being able to see things that others couldn't. That was the real reason she avoided the crystal.

"Well, let's see what a little focusing can do," she murmured. A nervous shiver shook her as a sliver of fear worked its way through her. Her chin firmed with resolve. "Time to see if this is a curse or a blessing," she told herself.

Her gaze leveled on the sphere. "I'm looking for my Mr. Right," she said firmly.

A face began to take shape. Her body tensed. It was Thatcher. Then another image began to appear in front of him. It was Laura.

"Thanks for nothing," she grumbled at the crystal. "Even *you* know that Thatcher's not available, so why show him to me?"

The images simply grew stronger. There was a sadness in Thatcher's eyes that reminded her of a man trapped in grief.

"This was a really stupid idea," she seethed at herself and turning abruptly away, she went back to Thatcher's.

That evening, as she sat in the living room trying to read the paper but listening to him playing with his children, she hoped they wouldn't ask her to join them. It had become common practice for them to seek her out when they needed a fourth player for one of their games or when Johnny wanted to play check-

ers or cards with his father and the two males wanted
a diversion for Melissa. Normally she didn't mind. But
tonight she felt the need for time away from Thatcher
and his children.

*I was beginning to want too much to belong with
them,* she sighed tiredly. *And that kind of wanting can
only lead to pain.*

Too restless to read, she folded the paper and set it
aside. Telling Maude that she was going for a walk,
she left the house. As she strolled down the tree-lined
streets, regret mingled with frustration. She wanted a
home and family more than she'd ever been willing to
admit. Returning to Thatcher's place, she still felt too
stressed out to go inside. So she sat on the rail, leaned
against a pillar and gazed up at the moon. There had
to be a Mr. Right for her—someone other than
Thatcher.

"The kids asked me to tell you good-night for
them."

Samantha's entire body tensed as Thatcher joined
her on the porch.

"We went looking for you when it was their bedtime, but Maude said you'd gone for a walk," he
continued in an easy drawl as he took his spot on the
rail.

His voice had been casual, but he was studying her
with an intensity that made her nerves even more taut.
"I'm sorry I missed saying good-night to them," she
said. That was the truth; she loved getting their hugs.
Leaving this house was going to be difficult.

"Is something wrong?" he asked bluntly. "You
seem on edge tonight." He frowned. "In fact, you've
seemed on edge all evening. Are you getting tired of
looking after my family? I know you're used to being

on your own. Guess it must be a strain to suddenly have four people to feed and clean up after."

The fear that if she stayed longer she would grow so attached to his family it would rip her apart to leave washed over her. She was tempted to tell him that taking care of all of them was a strain and she wanted out. Leaving now would be the smart thing to do. But she couldn't make herself do it. "I really don't mind looking after you and your family," she replied honestly.

He looked relieved. "Glad to hear that. You've fitted in here a lot better than I ever thought possible."

"I've fitted in a whole lot better than *I* ever thought possible," she admitted. Suddenly afraid of revealing too much if this line of conversation continued, she quickly changed the subject. "Has anyone reported seeing Luther?"

"No one," he replied. "With any luck he'll stay away."

Again she felt a rush of fear for Thatcher. Searching for a way to assure herself that he was a strong man who could take care of himself, she let her gaze travel over him. Neither of them had turned on the porch light. The only illumination was the moon and the bit of light filtering out through the lace-covered windows of the house. But although his features were shadowed, she could still see the firm line of his jaw. Her attention traveled to his broad shoulders, then down over his chest. His slacks were taut against the sturdy columns of his legs. A heat ignited within her, and she pulled her gaze away from him. "It's been a long day," she said, deciding that escaping from his company would be best. "I think I'll call it a night."

But as she rose, he rose, also. Reaching her in two long strides, he blocked her retreat. "I was wondering if you really meant what you said to Olivia about me—about revising your opinion of me."

Not wanting him to guess how much her feelings toward him had changed, she gave a nonchalant shrug. "I've decided that you're not quite the brutish bore I thought you were."

He smiled crookedly. "You're not the shrew I thought you were, either."

Samantha cursed silently. When he smiled that way she was lost. "I suppose coming from you I should consider that a compliment," she replied in a bantering tone as if his words had little or no effect on her.

His eyes darkened. "And you have the cutest little way of wrinkling your nose when you're uncertain."

His face was moving closer to hers. Her breath locked in her lungs. He actually looked as if he was going to kiss her. *That's a ridiculous thought,* she chided herself.

Thatcher cupped her face in his hands. "And I appreciate the protectiveness you show toward my children. It eases my mind to know they have you looking after them."

Disbelief held her motionless as his mouth moved closer to hers. *This is crazy,* she told herself. Still, her entire body was tense with anticipation.

At first the contact was so light it was like the touch of a butterfly. But even so, the heat seemed to scorch her. Every fiber of her being was aware of him. When he deepened the kiss, her legs weakened and her hands came up to his shoulders for support. The imprint of his muscles burned into her palms sending currents of excitement racing through her.

His fingers worked their way into her hair as he gently ran his thumbs along her jaw. It was as if his touch erased all sanity and in its place came a rush of pleasure.

Suddenly he released her. Her eyes opened as he stepped back out of her reach.

"Sorry," he apologized gruffly. "I shouldn't have done that." Self-directed anger was evident on his face and in his voice, adding proof that he regretted his action. Before she had a chance to respond, he strode into the house, leaving her alone on the porch.

He must have had a sudden surge of loneliness, she decided, fighting against the urge to cry out in sheer frustration. *I guess living with a ghost can leave a void where physical needs are concerned.*

She reseated herself on the porch railing. Her hands were shaking. She scowled. His embarrassment and quick retreat made it obvious he considered her the last person he would place on his list of possible romantic interests. "If he hadn't realized who he was kissing, this attraction you feel toward him could have proved disastrous," she murmured.

A flush of embarrassment began to creep up her neck as the incident replayed itself in her mind. She had practically melted in his arms. The flush reddened her cheeks. Once the shock of what he'd done wore off, he was certain to realize she'd displayed no resistance. How could she face him?

Suddenly the door opened and she heard his booted footsteps on the porch. Her back muscles knotted. He was probably going to say he'd look for someone to replace her as soon as possible. And that would be for the best, she told herself as just knowing that he was approaching caused a heat to spread through her.

Forcing an expression of indifference onto her face, she turned to look at him as he came to a halt a couple of feet away.

"I know what happened between us a few minutes ago was as much of a shock to you as it was to me," he said stiffly. A sheepish half grin played at one corner of his mouth. "I guess I'm lucky you didn't have time to react, or I'd probably have a black eye."

Samantha breathed a mental sigh of relief. He thought her lack of resistance had been because she'd been so startled.

"I can't blame you if you're considering quitting your job here," he continued, the grin replaced by a look of self-reproach. "I just want to assure you that if you'll stay, I'll keep my distance."

If I was smart, I'd grab this opportunity to leave, she told herself. *But I can't desert Maude and the kids,* she countered quickly. Aloud she heard herself saying, "A full moon has been known to cause people to behave irrationally."

"Especially in this town," Thatcher muttered, glancing up at the bright orb in the sky.

Puzzled by the intensity of the underlying current of perplexity in his voice, Samantha studied his taut profile. *Another mistake!* her inner voice screamed at her. The urge to run her fingers along the line of his jaw was nearly overwhelming. Immediately she jerked her gaze away. *You've got to stop overreacting to him,* she ordered herself. "I've heard that police all over the country claim they have more trouble on nights when there's a full moon than on any other night of the month."

"Heard that myself," he replied, returning his attention to her. "Anyway, I hope you'll forgive me and believe me when I say you don't have to worry about my making any more unwanted passes."

His tone left no doubt that he meant what he said. It was as if he considered his action horrendous. The sting of having been insulted was strong. She wanted to scream at him that she wasn't a toad, and he wouldn't get warts from having kissed her. But instead, she said coolly, "I suggest we forget it ever happened."

He nodded and relief spread over his features. "Consider it forgotten," he replied. Already moving toward the door, he added a quick good-night over his shoulder and went back inside.

"He can't seem to get away from me fast enough," she muttered, gazing up at the moon. A promise glistened in her eyes. "And that's the way I intend to feel toward him from this moment on."

Chapter Seven

Her promise was easier to make than to keep, she realized a little more than a week later.

"And I can't believe I'm doing this again," she murmured. It was nearly two in the morning and she was sitting in the kitchen staring at the clock, with a cup of what had been warm milk half an hour earlier cradled in her hands. Almost two hours ago, the phone had rung. As he had done a couple of weeks ago, Thatcher had knocked on the door of Maude's room, then stuck his head inside to tell Samantha he had to go out for a while.

After that, she'd tried to go back to sleep but, like the last time, she couldn't. Instead she'd lain in bed worrying about him. Finally she'd gotten up, put on her robe and slippers and came down to the kitchen, hoping some warm milk would help her relax. But her stomach had been too knotted for her to drink any.

She couldn't stop worrying that Luther had come back to town and that Thatcher might be in danger.

"It's probably just old Mrs. Elberly's cat. It probably knocked over something in her living room and she thinks she had a burglar and insisted that Thatcher come over with his deputy," she reasoned aloud. Scowling at herself, she wished she'd asked Thatcher where he was going and why, but that really wasn't any of her business. "I'm *not* his wife," she reminded herself curtly.

They were barely friendly. Not that there was any overt hostility between them. But since the incident on the porch, Thatcher had maintained his distance. They still ate their meals together and he continued to ask her to join him and the children in the evenings, but he made a point of never being alone with her. And although it wasn't anything she could actually touch, she sensed a barrier between them as strong as a steel wall.

"Go to bed before he comes in," she ordered herself for the umteenth time. Still, she sat looking at the clock.

The minute hand shifted to nineteen past one and her nerves grew more on edge. Then she heard the sound of his car pulling into the drive. She rose and, going over to the sink, poured her milk down the drain, then began washing out the pan.

"Anything wrong?" he asked gruffly, as he entered and hung his hat on a peg near the door.

"Just having a little trouble sleeping," she replied, not looking at him as she dried the pan and put it away. "Thought I'd try a little warm milk." She'd been avoiding looking at him, but now she glanced at him just to assure herself he was all right. Other than

a few tired lines etched into his face, he looked fine.
"Mrs. Elberly's cat?" she asked.

"Mary Conley thought she saw someone lurking outside her house. But if there was anyone, he left before we got there," he replied.

Samantha felt a cold shaft of fear shoot through her. "Luther Conley has a cruel streak. I don't blame her for being edgy."

Thatcher nodded his agreement.

He was watching her from behind a shuttered gaze. Suddenly his mask slipped and she saw anger mingled with frustration in his eyes.

"Dammit, Samantha," he growled. "I'm only human and you're one inviting-looking woman."

His words stunned her. She'd glanced at herself in the mirror as she'd passed through the hall earlier. Her hair was mussed, there were dark circles under her eyes and her old robe was definitely in the frumpy category. She looked, she'd thought, like something the cat had dragged in. But there was a heat in his gaze that told her he didn't see her that way; he saw her more as a tasty morsel. The thought that he might want to take a bite filled her with excitement. *Fool!* she screamed at herself, but she made no attempt to flee. Her breath caught and she stood frozen, waiting for him to make the next move.

For one brief moment, she was sure he was going to approach her, then he abruptly turned and stalked out of the kitchen.

"He might be attracted, but he clearly considers me unsuitable," she murmured, the sting of insult again sharp. "Well, I've always known he was bullheaded. Obviously he made a decision years ago that I wasn't the kind of woman he could fall in love with, and he's determined to stick to it. Beneath that I-try-to-be-a-fair-man exterior is a small-minded hypocrite who refuses to admit he can make an error.'' Her chin firmed. Well, she had no use for a man like that. *My original evaluation of him as a boor was correct,* she told herself. With that thought in mind, she went up to bed.

The next morning, the barrier she sensed Thatcher kept between them was even stronger. She assured herself it didn't bother her. Now that she understood the real man, she had no more interest in him than he had in her. What did disturb her was the evident discomfort her presence caused him. From the moment he walked into the kitchen, he avoided looking at her or getting near her. His behavior, however, was subtle and she was the only one who noticed.

Or maybe I'm just overreacting, she mused about midmorning. Although she now knew he considered her a necessary irritant, she doubted that she occupied enough of his thoughts to actually cause him any real discomfort. *He probably just didn't get enough sleep and was on edge,* she decided.

But when he called to say he wouldn't be coming home for lunch, she knew she was wrong. *It's time for me to leave,* she told herself. This was his home, and she wouldn't remain and inflict herself on him any longer.

''I want you to find someone to take over for me. I've decided I should start looking for a more permanent job,'' she informed Maude during the noonday meal. ''I appreciate your giving me this temporary position, and I've enjoyed taking care of you and the children, but I'm feeling anxious. I need to know I have a job that I can support myself with for the long term.''

"Have you and Thatcher had a fight I don't know about?'' Maude questioned sharply.

"No, we haven't fought,'' she replied honestly.

Maude regarded her thoughtfully. "I can understand your wanting to begin looking for another job, but wouldn't it be more practical to keep this one while you search?''

"I'm thinking of going to Boston to look.'' This thought hadn't crossed Samantha's mind until she spoke the words. Now it sounded like a terrific idea. *You're running away from Thatcher,* her inner voice scolded. *I'm looking for a new beginning,* she rebutted, refusing to admit he could run her out of town.

Maude sighed resignedly. "I don't relish finding someone else to take your place, but if you feel you must go, then I'll start looking. I'll need a couple of days.''

Maude was actually being agreeable! Samantha felt as if a weight had been lifted from her shoulders. "That's fine. I'll need to make a few arrangements myself.''

This was definitely for the best, she told herself a little later. Melissa was taking her afternoon nap and Johnny was playing checkers with Howard. Samantha had taken this opportunity to go next door to her own house. With each passing moment, the thought of going to Boston had grown more and more appealing. Now she was standing in front of the closet in her bedroom surveying her wardrobe and deciding what she should pack. "And I'm not running away from Thatcher,'' she reaffirmed. There wasn't anything to run away *from.* He wasn't interested in her, and she certainly wasn't interested in him now that she knew the real man.

"There simply isn't any future for me here other than spinsterhood," she continued philosophically. "None of the available males appeals to me. Boston should be full of prospects, and even if I don't find a man to share my life, I'll find more adventure than I would staying here. Staying here, I'll end up a spinster in a very narrow rut."

The ringing of the front doorbell caused her to jump. All thoughts of Boston vanished. Concern that Howard had come looking for her because one of the children had been injured filled her mind. Hurrying downstairs, she flung open the door—and gasped in surprise.

"My mother called to tell me you were talking about going to Boston," Thatcher said, opening the screen door and entering.

Samantha took a step back to keep some distance between them. A rush of anger swept through her. She had no feelings for him any longer. There was no reason for her to be intimidated by his presence. "I've been thinking that it's time I looked for a permanent job."

"Maybe looking for another job would be for the best," he agreed stiffly. "But Boston can be a dangerous city for a woman alone."

She glared at him. He was patronizing her! "I can take care of myself," she assured him coolly.

For a moment he regarded her in silence, then said, "You've got a house, and your family is here. Surely you can find a job in Smytheshire to suit you."

She saw him shift his shoulders slightly as he spoke. He was obviously uncomfortable talking to her. It occurred to her that Maude had probably insisted he come. "There's no reason for pretense between us. I know you would be glad to see me go," she said.

His expression became shuttered. "I don't dislike having you around."

Her nerves, already taut, snapped at this lie. "I'm not blind. You can barely stand to be in the same room with me."

He scowled. "It's not you. It's me. I'm attracted to you."

Samantha glared at him. He was again admitting that he found her appealing, but he'd made this admission in a tone of self-disgust. "Worse things could happen to a man," she said dryly.

Taking his hat off, he raked his hand agitatedly through his hair. "You don't understand." He paced down the hall away from her, then paced back. Coming to a halt, he said grimly, "Laura died because of me. With her parents having been killed in that car crash when she was still a teenager and her only living grandparents having moved to California, she only had me to protect her. I failed."

The depth of guilt in his voice shook her. "Laura died in childbirth. It's tragic, but it happens," she said in soothing tones.

The self-recrimination in his tone increased. "She should never have gotten pregnant a second time. The doctor warned her it would be dangerous."

He looked so distraught Samantha wanted to put her arms around him and comfort him. But she could still sense the wall he'd erected between them, and she knew he did not want her to touch him. "Laura and I used to talk over the back fence quite a bit," she said.

"She probably never mentioned that to you, because she knew how much you disapproved of me."

He shifted uneasily. "I knew you two talked."

Mentally she visualized him warning Laura that she would be wise to stay away from Samantha. But the anger this vision would normally have caused was missing. The pain in his eyes was so intense it was impossible for her to feel anything other than sympathy for him. "Laura told me several times that she wanted a second child. In fact, she was adamant about it," Samantha said. "And when she did get pregnant, I had the feeling it was more her choice than yours. In fact, I recall her telling me that you weren't all that happy about the pregnancy in the beginning."

"Because I knew how dangerous it was for her," he replied. His expression grew even grimmer. "During her pregnancy with Johnny, Doc James discovered that, in her case, having a child put more strain on her heart than he felt was safe. He advised her against having any more children. We discussed the possibility of her having a tubal ligation. But Laura didn't like the idea of going in for surgery, and Doc James admitted that he was somewhat uneasy about putting her under anesthetic. Her condition was erratic, unpredictable."

He looked so wretched Samantha wanted to cry for him. "Then Laura's pregnancy with Melissa was an accident because the birth-control you were using failed?"

She was about to point out that he couldn't blame himself for an accident like that when he said grimly, "No, nothing failed. Laura got pregnant on purpose."

Samantha frowned at him in confusion. "Then I don't understand why you blame yourself."

"She thought *I* wanted another child," he growled, self-accusation resounding in his voice. "I told her I was perfectly happy with one child, but she didn't believe me. I should have had a vasectomy. That would have convinced her. But I didn't. Maybe down deep I did want more children, I don't know. All I know is that I got her pregnant, and it killed her."

His anguish tore at her. "Laura loved you. She wouldn't want you to torture yourself this way."

"She loved me and I loved her. But our love cost Laura her life." His jaw hardened with resolve. "She deserves my undying faithfulness and loyalty."

"And you feel that by being attracted to me you're betraying her," Samantha said, as the full implication of all he had told her hit her.

He nodded. A flush of embarrassment suddenly reddened his neck. "Considering the fact I'm most likely the last man on earth you'd be attracted to, this must seem like a tempest in a teapot to you."

He'd be shocked if he knew just how attracted to him she was, she thought. But he wouldn't want to hear that. "I've discovered that you have a few good points," she replied with schooled nonchalance.

His expression became solemn. "I hope you'll reconsider and stay. The kids have grown fond of you and Maude's comfortable with you. As for me, I'll try not to be so boorish."

The smart thing to do would be to head straight to Boston, her inner voice counseled. Instead, she heard herself saying, "I suppose I could put off looking for a new job until Maude's leg is healed."

Relief spread over his face. "Thanks." Then, as if feeling the need to make a quick escape, he strode toward the door, adding over his shoulder, "I'd better be getting back to work. See you around five."

"Around five," she echoed.

Standing alone in the foyer, she breathed a heavy sigh. "You're a fool to stay," she berated the image staring back at her in the mirror. "You saw the look on his face. He's never going to get over Laura."

Shoving her hands into the pockets of her jeans, she paced into the living room. She really didn't have a choice, she reasoned. She had to stay. Leaving now would seem petty and uncaring. Besides, she'd already agreed to remain.

Looking out the window, she saw him exiting his house and walking toward his patrol car. The memory of his kiss assailed her and sent a heat surging through her. Resolve spread across her face. *He's worth fighting for.* Abruptly the resolve was replaced by indecision. The problem, she mused, was how to go about the wooing of Thatcher Brant.

Closing her eyes, she saw his face. Grief mingled with guilt in his features. He looked like a man who could use a friend. Her eyes opened. That was as good a place as any to start; she would work at being his friend.

Her gaze shifted to the crystal sphere. It seemed to be glowing slightly with a pale pink tint. Approaching it, she was fairly certain what she would see and it didn't disappoint her. Inside was the same image she had seen before. Laura stood in the foreground with Thatcher behind her, like a sentinel designed to keep Thatcher and Samantha apart.

Determination flashed in Samantha's eyes. "I won't give him up without a fight."

But that night as she tossed and turned in bed, too restless to sleep, she had her doubts about winning this war. All evening, Thatcher had been polite but distant. The wall he kept between the two of them seemed even thicker than before. *You knew it wouldn't be easy,* she reminded herself. *Just take it slow. One step at a time. Think "friendship,"* she ordered herself.

The next morning, instead of matching his coolness toward her, she maintained an unruffled even-tempered demeanor. She didn't want to act actually friendly just yet. That would be sure to scare him off.

Once, she caught him watching her with an uneasy guarded expression on his face. Immediately he turned his attention to Melissa.

At least he hasn't been able to make himself totally ignore the fact that I'm here, she told herself encouragingly.

But later that morning she began to have her doubts about her plan of action. He'd admitted he was attracted to her, but that attraction could be purely physical, she cautioned herself. After all, she was now sure he hadn't been with a woman since Laura. *And if this attraction he feels to me is only physical, I could get hurt badly if I break down his barrier and then he gets tired of me,* she warned herself.

But at noon, as she stood at the kitchen window watching him walk to the back door, she knew she wasn't going to give up on him.

"How was your morning?" she asked as he entered the kitchen.

"Uneventful," he replied.

His tone let her know he didn't want to talk. Normally she would have dropped the attempt at conversation right there. But she'd made up her mind to force at least one more remark out of him. She couldn't build a friendship between them if she allowed their exchanges to continue on a cursory level. If each day she forced him to say a little more than he had the day before, eventually they would have a real conversation. "Considering your line of work, that's good," she returned with the barest hint of banter in her voice.

"True," he replied, continuing through the kitchen and out into the hall.

"It looks like just getting him to pause for a moment when I'm the only person in the room is going to be my first challenge," she muttered under her breath.

During lunch she studied him covertly. When he spoke to Maude or the children, he relaxed and a softness came into his eyes. But the moment his attention shifted to her, he became guarded. *You knew this wouldn't be easy,* she reminded herself.

But later that evening, she had to admit that getting past the wall he'd built around himself was beginning to look totally impossible. She was in the kitchen washing the dinner dishes. The children were in the den playing. Maude was there keeping an eye on them and reading the paper while she waited for Howard to arrive. Thatcher had been standing alone on the back porch. Howard had arrived, but instead of immediately joining Maude, he'd sought out Thatcher.

Samantha didn't normally eavesdrop on other people's conversations, but the weather was warm, the windows and back door were open and the men's voices floated in.

"I have to admit I'm disappointed that you and Samantha aren't getting along all that well," Howard said bluntly, after exchanging a cursory greeting with Thatcher.

Through the window, Samantha saw Thatcher's jaw tense as he glanced at the older man. "We're getting along just fine," he replied coolly.

"I was hoping you two would get along better than fine," Howard continued. "The two of you have always reacted so strongly to one another I was hoping those hostile sparks might change to something different once you got to know one another a little better. Even caught you looking at her one evening in a way that made me think you might be seeing her in a more attractive light."

"There aren't any sparks, hostile or otherwise, between me and Samantha," Thatcher said firmly.

"I guess what I'm really getting at," Howard persisted, "is that you're still a young man. Laura's been gone better than two years now. It's time you got on with your life."

"I am getting on with my life. I'm just not looking to get married again, if that's what you're driving at," Thatcher growled. It was clear he thought Howard was trespassing in territory where he didn't belong.

Samantha stood practically not breathing. The dishes were forgotten as she stared out the window at the two men, waiting for what Howard would say next. Most men would have been cowed by Thatcher's manner, but she noticed that Howard simply squared his shoulders and faced the younger man squarely. "Guess I'm being a bit selfish," he said. "I love your mother. I want to marry her."

Thatcher studied the older man. "How does my mother feel about you?"

"She cares for me. But I also know how strong an obligation she feels toward you and your children. If you were married, had a wife to look after you and be a mother to your children, I feel pretty confident I'd have a chance of convincing Maude to marry me."

"Like I just said, I'm not looking to find another wife," Thatcher repeated firmly. Then his tone softened. "But I don't want my mother feeling trapped in a situation she isn't happy in."

"I'm not saying she isn't happy here with you," Howard said quickly. "She loves you and your children."

"I know. But she deserves a life of her own." Thatcher held out his hand to Howard. "I appreciate your telling me how you feel. I'll have a talk with her."

Samantha's morale dropped a notch as she watched the two shake hands. The conviction in Thatcher's voice when he'd said he didn't want another wife was enough to halt the most ardent optimist.

Her gaze shifted back to the dishes. *But then I've never been a quitter,* she told herself, *and I'm not going to become one now.*

Later that evening after Howard left, Samantha sat on the porch waiting. The children were already tucked in bed. Normally she would have been helping Maude with her bedtime routine, but true to his word, Thatcher had sought out his mother to have a mother-son talk.

Closing her eyes, she tried to envision Thatcher smiling at her, Samantha Hogan, the way he smiled at his children. But she couldn't erase the guardedness from his face. *Maybe the barrier would weaken if I tried to be more like Laura,* she thought. *But she'd never been the Pollyanna type, and even for Thatcher she couldn't live a lie.*

"I've already helped my mother up to her room. She's waiting there for you." Samantha jumped slightly as Thatcher's voice broke into her thoughts.

She couldn't tell from his expression how his conversation with his mother had gone. And she couldn't ask. Not only would that be prying, but it would also be an admission she'd eavesdropped on him and Howard. "Thanks," she said simply, and quickly went inside. Reaching Maude's room, she found the older woman on the phone.

"Samantha's here. I'll talk to you tomorrow," Maude said lovingly into the receiver, then hung up.

As Maude looked up at her, the depth of concern on the older woman's face shook Samantha. "Is something wrong?" Samantha asked anxiously.

"I hope not," Maude replied. "I'm just not sure." She blushed and a smile tilted the corners of her mouth. "Howard wants me to marry him."

"That's wonderful!" Samantha said encouragingly. Knowing the turmoil Maude had to be going through and wanting to give her a chance to talk if she wanted, she added with concern, "It is wonderful, isn't it?"

The smile on Maude's face widened. "Yes. Yes, it is," she replied. Then her smile faded and the worried expression returned. "And Thatcher has told me that he wants me to be happy, and he's assured me that if I want to marry Howard it's fine with him. He says he'll hire a housekeeper to take care of him and the children. In fact, he says he's going to start looking tomorrow. He's insistent that I lead my own life.''

"He's right. You *should* lead your own life," Samantha said with conviction, attempting to alleviate some of Maude's anxiety. "And I'm sure Thatcher can find a suitable housekeeper."

Maude sighed. "I'd hoped he would find a wife." Her gaze leveled on Samantha. "Howard and I had been talking about getting married when Laura died. I broke off with him because I knew Thatcher needed me. But I've missed Howard. When he started visiting me regularly after I injured my leg, I just couldn't send him away again."

"And Thatcher wouldn't want you to," Samantha assured her.

But Maude didn't look convinced. "To be perfectly honest, I had an ulterior motive in demanding that you be hired to take care of me." She grimaced self-consciously. "I know you'll think I'm being ridiculous, but I like you and I've been harboring the notion that if you and Thatcher were forced to spend some time together, you might begin to see each other in a different light—you might even discover you like each other." She paused and looked reminiscent. "Sort of like the revelation Howard and I had. We'd been neighbors for years and considered each other friendly acquaintances, but nothing more. Then one day those goats of his got out again. Every time they managed to break free, they always made a beeline for my vegetable garden. I wasn't in a good mood that day. When I found them there eating my plants, I was furious. Howard drove up just then, and I let him know what I thought of his animals. Suddenly he said, 'You've got fire in you, Maude Brant. I like that.' Well, that stopped me cold. I found myself blushing for the first time in years and he just stood there grinning. The next thing I knew he was asking me out on a date and I was accepting.''

As much as Samantha wanted Thatcher to allow her to become a real part of his life, her honest side had to admit her chances were slim. She recalled the resolute sound of his voice when he'd told Howard he was not looking for a wife. Now he'd told Maude he'd start looking for a housekeeper tomorrow. Samantha wasn't ready to give up entirely, but she also wasn't going to try to fool herself. "I doubt that what you and Howard have found together is ever going to happen between me and Thatcher," she said evenly, as much for her own ears as for Maude's.

Maude nodded. "I know. Still, I've been hoping that simply having a young woman around would make him see what he's missing." She sighed. "I didn't realize what a strong hold Laura continues to have on him."

And may always have on him, Samantha thought glumly.

"Anyway," Maude continued, a coaxing quality entering her voice, "I have to know for certain that Thatcher doesn't think I'm deserting him. Will you talk to him, find out how he really feels?"

"I'm sure he's happy for you," Samantha replied. She was walking on eggshells where Thatcher was concerned. She wanted to become his friend. Now Maude was asking her to pry.

"Please, just talk to him?" Maude pleaded. "I can't even enjoy the *thought* of marrying Howard until I know Thatcher is honestly happy for me."

Samantha felt trapped. Maude was her friend. And most likely, she'd never break down Thatcher's barrier, anyway. "All right," she agreed.

After helping Maude into bed, she went in search of Thatcher. He was seated in his usual spot on the porch rail. "Maude told me about her and Howard," she said, watching him closely.

He frowned. "I feel like a heel. I wish she'd told me about their relationship when Laura died. I can't believe I broke them up. I never realized how close they'd grown. I thought they were just friends back then."

"Maude doesn't regret having moved in here to take care of you and your kids," she assured him. She'd considered approaching him subtly about his real feelings, but it was more in her nature to be blunt. Besides, she reasoned, it was the real her she wanted him to accept as a friend and then, she hoped, learn to care deeply for. "However, she is worried you might think she's deserting you."

"I've already told her I don't think that," he said.

The honesty in his voice rang true. She nodded with approval. "I told her you wanted her to be happy. But she insisted I try to find out how you *really* feel. Now I can ease her mind."

Thatcher leaned back against the pillar, his gaze shifting to the clear night sky. "Howard is a lucky man. They're both lucky. Life can get real lonely when you don't have someone to share it with.''

Samantha felt a spark of hope.

Abruptly he stiffened as if just then realizing what he'd said. Guilt spread over his face, then his expression became shuttered. "I think I should go tell her myself one more time how happy I am for her."

As he passed Samantha, the hard set of his jaw caused the spark of hope in her to die. *You're fighting a loosing battle,* her inner voice warned.

Chapter Eight

By noon the next day, Samantha felt as if she'd been caught in a whirlwind.

After Thatcher's second talk with Maude the night before, Maude had called Howard and accepted his proposal.

"We've wasted too much time as it is," Howard had said. "I want to tie the knot as quickly as possible."

Thatcher had agreed with him and promised to step up his search for a housekeeper.

Maude had been agreeable to setting a date that wasn't too far into the future. But she'd insisted on being able to walk down the aisle. This morning, Maude had paid a visit to Dr. Prescott. He'd said the leg seemed to be healing well and thought the cast could come off in about four weeks. They'd settled on a date for that event. Then Maude had set the date of the wedding for two days later.

Now Samantha was busy helping her make arrangements for the wedding. As they decided on a guest list and began planning the reception, Samantha couldn't stop thinking about Thatcher and wishing she were planning her wedding to him. *Don't go getting your hopes up,* her inner voice warned. She knew her chances of breaking down the barrier he was determined to keep around his heart were slim, but she wasn't ready to give up on him yet.

That evening after the children and Maude were tucked in for the night, she sought him out. "Sounds as if you're getting a good start on your search for a housekeeper," she said, referring to the conversation between him and his mother during dinner. He'd told Maude he'd spread the word he was looking for someone to come live in his home and take care of him and his children. He'd also rattled off a list of women he considered possible candidates for the job. Maude had come up with a few more names.

"Yeah," he replied, glancing at Samantha and then looking back up at the sky.

It was obvious he didn't want to talk. Still she made herself persist. "Thought I heard you on the phone making appointments to meet with a few of those women you had on your list."

"Yeah," he replied again, this time not even looking at her.

One more try, she ordered herself. "Telling Mabel Baker was an inspired move," she said. "I'll bet that within a couple of hours everyone in and around Smytheshire knew you were looking for a housekeeper. Considering Mabel's ability to spread the word, they probably knew all the way to Greenfield."

"Probably," he replied. Yawning, he rose and stretched. "It's been a long day. Think I'll go to bed."

Alone on the porch, she considered giving up. *Not yet,* she told herself firmly.

The next night, she sought him out again. And again he answered in monosyllables and avoided looking at her. After a few minutes, he announced he was feeling restless and went for a walk. She considered tagging along, but that, she decided, would have been too pushy. He hadn't asked for her company, and she knew she wasn't invited.

Are you ready to give up now? her inner voice asked as she watched his departing back for the second night in a row. *Not quite yet,* she answered, but she had to admit her hope was dying fast.

At least I have something to tell him that should interest him, she told herself when she sought him out the next night.

"I think Johnny has been considering the advantages of having Howard for a grandfather," she said as she stepped out onto the porch.

At the mention of his son, Thatcher's gaze swung to her. "He has?"

At least he was looking at her, she thought. "Yes, I'm pretty sure he has big plans for his birthday gift," she continued with a warm smile.

Thatcher studied her. "And just what are his plans?"

"I think he wants a pony," she replied.

Thatcher grinned crookedly. "A pony?"

Samantha's heart skipped a beat. He looked so boyishly handsome. *Don't let him guess the effect he's having on you,* she warned herself curtly. *That would be sure to scare him off.* "Earlier this afternoon he was asking Howard if Howard had enough room on his farm for another animal," she explained, keeping her tone warm but not *too* warm. "When Howard said he thought he could handle another one, Johnny asked if Howard would mind if he kept a pet out there. Then, while I was fixing dinner, Johnny came in to see me and was telling me about how you had a pony when you were a child."

Thatcher laughed gently. "Guess I'd better have a talk with Howard myself, and if he agrees, I'll start checking into available livestock. When that boy sets his mind to something, he rarely changes it."

"I've noticed that," Samantha replied, smiling, also. The thought that maybe there was hope, after all, began to grow as she realized they were actually having a friendly exchange.

"I appreciate the advance warning," Thatcher said.

He was looking at her. Steeling herself, she met his gaze. Her breath caught in her throat. She was sure she saw a longing in his eyes.

Abruptly his jaw tensed with purpose. He rose and moved toward her. When he was still a couple of feet away, he stopped. "I'm going to miss having you around," he said gruffly, then he turned away and strode into the house.

"He and Johnny are definitely cut from the same cloth," she murmured sadly. "Once their minds are set on something, nothing short of a miracle will change it."

The next evening, after she had all of her charges tucked in bed, she didn't seek out Thatcher. Instead, she went into the kitchen. "All right, so I'm giving up," she confessed to her shadowy image in the win-

dow as she ran water into the teakettle. All day she'd
held a running argument with herself. But no amount
of optimism could erase the finality of his parting
words the evening before. He'd made it clear he had
no intention of keeping her in his life.

She took down a mug then found a teabag. The
thought of moving to Boston was growing more appealing by the moment. "I always knew that if anyone could run me out of this town it would be
Thatcher Brant," she mused dryly.

The kettle began to spout steam. Absently she
turned off the burner, poured the water into the mug,
then set the kettle back on the stove. She wanted to
scream in frustration.

"Are you feeling ill?"

She twisted around to see Thatcher entering the
kitchen. The gruff concern in his voice shook her.
"No," she managed to choke out, hope once again
washing over her.

"Just thought I'd check," he said, the concern replaced by a cool businesslike demeanor. "Guess I've
gotten so used to you coming out to join me for a few
minutes, I got a little anxious when you didn't—sort
of like waiting for the second shoe to drop."

The barrier was as strong as ever, she thought as she
watched him remaining near the door. Even more disconcerting, she could almost feel his desire to escape
from her presence. "Consider it dropped," she replied frostily.

He nodded. "I've got a few phone calls to make,"
he said and in the next moment had eased himself out
of the room.

Her jaw tensed. If the man wanted to live with a
ghost, she'd let him.

* * *

"Leona Boggs came by the office today," Thatcher said as they all sat eating dinner the next evening. "She says that since her children are all busy with their own families and her husband has died, she's lonely in that big old house of hers. She says she's looking to earn a little extra money so she can travel a bit. But more importantly, she says she needs to feel needed, so she's applying for the job here as housekeeper."

"She's a nice woman," Samantha commented, telling herself she would be relieved when he actually hired someone to replace her. She had promised Maude she would stay until Maude's cast came off, and she was committed to helping with the wedding. But as soon as Maude and Howard had said their vows, she never intended to cross the threshold of this house again. True, she would hate leaving Melissa and Johnny, but she had no choice. They were Thatcher's children and there was no place in his life for her. Well, maybe she would find a few chances to visit with the children when he wasn't around, she amended, unable to face the thought of totally walking away from them. "Leona's energetic, mature, a definite mothering type," she finished.

Thatcher nodded. "I agree. And she's a good cook, except when she tries one of her experiments." He grimaced and Samantha couldn't blame him. Leona had described the casserole she'd brought to the last town social as adventurous, but that hadn't been how those who tasted it had described it. It had been some sort of Mexican dish to which she'd added so many hot spices and chilies Dr. James had joked about using it to clear everyone's sinuses.

"I'm sure you can convince her that the children should be fed nice plain food," Samantha said quickly.

Maude frowned with concern. "Maybe I could work out a schedule where I could continue to help you."

Smiling warmly, Thatcher took his mother's hand in his. "I appreciate everything you've done for me and the children, but now it's time for you and Howard to have some time to yourselves. And I think he'd agree with me."

Maude blushed. "We do have some catching up to do," she conceded. Then, her expression once again becoming serious, she said, "But you know you can call on us whenever you need us."

"I know," Thatcher replied.

"Why can't Samantha stay?" Johnny demanded abruptly.

Startled by his unexpected championing of her, Samantha looked at him. He was regarding the adults with the same impatient superior expression she'd seen on his father's face so many times before. She'd realized he'd begun to accept her as part of their household, but she'd thought that this was merely because his father had accepted her. She'd never let herself believe that the boy had actually grown as fond of her as she had of him.

"She's a good cook and she knows how to play all our games and she's fun to have around and Melissa and I like having her here," Johnny declared all in one breath. He glanced toward his sister.

"Samantha!" Melissa said enthusiastically, as if responding to a cue.

Watching the two of them, Samantha realized they had been talking about this privately. She'd known they were uneasy about all the changes that were going to take place in their lives. So that these wouldn't be a shock, she, Thatcher and Maude had talked openly to the children about Maude's upcoming marriage and the hiring of a new housekeeper. On a daily basis, Samantha had assured the children they would like whomever their father hired. But apparently the children had decided they wanted a say in what was happening.

"Samantha is trained to be a secretary, not a housekeeper," Thatcher stated, firmly dismissing the children's suggestion.

Johnny looked at her, a plea in his eyes. "You're a fast learner. You've said so yourself. I'm sure you would be the very best housekeeper in the world."

It had occurred to Samantha that the little boy wanted her to remain merely because he didn't want to have to face the changes a new housekeeper would make in his life. But the distress on his face told her she was wrong. He really *had* become attached to her. And now he was making her feel as if she was deserting him and his sister. But she had no choice. "My staying here once your grandmother is gone would cause gossip," she explained.

He frowned impatiently. "What's gossip?"

"It's when people tell stories about other people. Sometimes they're true, sometimes they're exaggerations of the truth, and sometimes they're out-and-out lies," Maude explained. She gave her grandson a regretful look. "Samantha is right. She's much too young and much too pretty to remain here once I'm gone."

Johnny scowled. Looking his grandmother directly in the eye, he demanded, "But didn't you say that we needed someone like Samantha to take care of Melissa and me?"

Mentally, Samantha smiled. Johnny was definitely a miniature version of his father. Once his mind was set, it took an act of congress to change it.

"Samantha cannot stay, and there is no sense in continuing this discussion," Thatcher said with finality before Maude had a chance to respond.

For a moment the boy looked as if he was going to challenge his father, but the set of Thatcher's jaw obviously convinced him that would not be a good idea.

Thatcher still gets top points for being the most obstinate, Samantha thought as she returned her attention to her food.

Melissa had been sitting quietly, but now she began to weep. "Samantha," she said pleadingly, holding her arms out in Samantha's direction.

Samantha saw Thatcher's jaw tense even more. Well, she hadn't planned this, she defended mentally. She'd simply learned to love his children and apparently they'd grown to care for her. "Don't cry, sweetheart," she said, lifting Melissa out of her chair and hugging her. "I'll come visit. And I'm sure your father will find someone who will be wonderful and you'll have great fun."

Tears continued to roll down Melissa's cheeks. "Want you!"

The determination in the child's voice was unwavering. *Thatcher's going to have his hands full when his children grow up,* Samantha thought. *He already has his hands full.* She experienced a rush of sympathy for the man. "Honestly, your father knows what's best," she said, her gaze shifting to encompass Johnny. Recalling how dubious he'd been when she'd first entered his home, she added, "You weren't so sure you wanted me here when I first came, and I worked out all right. The new housekeeper will work out just as well."

Johnny didn't look totally convinced, but he did look resigned. "Melissa, stop crying," he ordered gently. "Or Samantha won't even want to come back and visit."

Fear spread over Melissa's face and her weeping stopped. "Come back?" she said, staring into Samantha's face.

"Of course, I'll come back," she promised. *But only when Thatcher isn't here,* she added silently. Aloud she said, "Now, let's finish our dinner."

As Samantha returned Melissa to her chair, Thatcher attempted to lighten the mood at the table. "I've been thinking about driving out to see Martin Green," he said. "I hear he has a couple of ponies he's thinking about selling." He leveled his gaze on Johnny. "You interested in coming along?"

"I suppose," the boy replied, but the enthusiasm in his voice was restrained.

It was flattering to know that even a pony couldn't totally distract the boy's mind from her leaving, but Samantha also couldn't sit by and allow the evening to sour because of her. Injecting a note of envy into her voice, she said, "I wanted a pony when I was your age, but we lived in town." She turned her attention to Maude. "I'll bet there's a lot of places a person could ride on Howard's farm."

"And they'll have Brant land to ride on, too," Maude added, attempting to do her part.

Johnny's face brightened.

"Pony for me, too," Melissa said hopefully.

"You'll have to get a little older," Johnny informed her authoritatively. Then, turning to his father, he asked, "Do you really think you might get me one?"

"It's a possibility," Thatcher replied. "But we'll want to look around and see what's available before we make any firm decisions."

"Your dad's saddle is stored at my farm," Maude said, a reminiscent smile spreading across her face. "I recall he had a lot of happy adventures on his pony when he was a child."

"And some not so happy." Thatcher grinned. "I remember when I tried to teach Gray how to jump a fence. Took a real bruising that day until I decided that ponies weren't built for jumping."

The rest of the meal was filled with stories of Thatcher's childhood and his experiences with his pony.

Samantha joined in the laughter, but inside she experienced a deep sense of regret. She was going to miss this family very much. *I'm sure I can find a man who will love me and I'll love him, and we'll have a family as nice as this one,* she assured herself. *I just have to start looking harder.*

Much later that evening, after Maude and the children were in bed, Samantha wandered out onto the back porch. Seating herself in the one of the two large old rocking chairs, she gazed up at the night sky. She'd specifically chosen this spot to avoid running into Thatcher. At the moment, she knew he was in the den.

If he did decide to get a breath of fresh air, she was sure he would go out onto the front porch.

She felt a strong attachment to Smytheshire, but she knew now that she didn't want to live her life alone, and she wasn't going to find a husband here.

"Never thought I'd be bribing a son of mine with a pony to get him over his grief at losing you."

Samantha turned to see Thatcher stepping out onto the porch. "Guess that was a surprise," she managed to reply watching him as he walked over to one of the pillars and leaned against it. *It isn't fair for him to look so appealing,* she thought with a rush of frustration. Turning away, she tried to concentrate on the darkened landscape in front of her.

"Maude said you were still thinking about going to Boston," he said, breaking the silence that had fallen between them.

"Yes. I'm considering calling Madaline Darnell and seeing if she knows of any jobs for me," she replied. Unable to stop herself, she glanced at him again. A rush of heat swept through her. Immediately she jerked her attention away. Even if Madaline couldn't help her, she was definitely leaving town, at least for a while, she decided.

"I've never liked being in big cities." His expression grew grim. Straightening away from the post, he started toward the kitchen door. "But if that's what you want to do, then I wish you the best."

"Thanks," she replied to his departing back. Her mouth formed a pout. For one brief moment she'd actually held out the hope he might tell her he'd worry about her if she went and that he wanted her to stay here in Smytheshire...that he wanted her to stay with him. "I'm really hooked on him," she muttered with self-reproach. "The sooner I leave this town the better."

Samantha quickly learned that Johnny had not given up his attempt to have her stay. The next morning at breakfast, when Thatcher began making plans for taking Johnny to Martin Green's place, the boy suggested his sister come along. "Melissa wants to see the ponies," he said.

Samantha noticed him give his sister a slight nod.

"I come, too!" Melissa said immediately.

Looking down at her food, Samantha smiled softly. It was obvious Johnny had instructed his sister in what to say and when to say it. *Those two are going to be a handful,* she thought, *even for Thatcher Brant.*

"Sure, you can come," Thatcher agreed with a loving grin.

Samantha saw the gleam in Johnny's eyes. Whatever scheme the boy had in mind was clearly working.

"Since Melissa is coming, Samantha should probably come, too, just in case we need someone to watch Melissa while you and I look at the ponies," Johnny said with authority. Then as if not certain this was reason enough, he added, "Besides, Grandma says Samantha has good common sense, and that's important when making a decision."

Samantha frowned. So that was his game. He was going to force her down his father's throat. She glanced at Thatcher. He looked like a man snared in a trap. "I really need to stay here and take care of Maude," she said. "We've got a lot of planning left to do for the wedding. You three can have a nice little family outing."

Relief spread over Thatcher's face. "Samantha's right. We can't leave Maude here by herself."

"Howard could come stay with her," Johnny insisted, clearly not ready to give up easily. His gaze leveled on his father. "We really need Samantha."

Samantha's chin trembled at the edge of desperation in the boy's voice. She wanted to go to him, give him a hug and assure him she would always be around if he needed her, but that wouldn't be fair to Thatcher. Johnny wanted her in his life, but Thatcher didn't want her in his, and she wouldn't allow the children to force her presence on their father. "I'm sure you and your father can handle whatever problems arise and make whatever decisions have to be made," she said firmly. Unable to bear the hurt look of one who has been rejected that spread over Johnny's face, she added, "Besides, Howard can't help plan the wedding. That requires a woman's touch."

"Samantha's right." Maude came to Samantha's aid. "You don't want my wedding to be a flop, do you?"

"No," Johnny replied. He still didn't look happy, but apparently he was pacified, and the rest of the meal passed peaceably.

When they had finished eating, the children went into the den to play while Maude went into the living room to go over the list of what still needed to be done for the wedding.

As Samantha began clearing the table, Thatcher came back through the kitchen on his way out of the house. Pausing in the doorway, he turned toward her. "It would appear you're going to be much harder to replace than I'd anticipated," he said.

The edge of accusation in his voice caused her to stiffen. "I didn't plan for your children to grow so attached to me."

He drew a terse breath. "I didn't say you did." For a brief moment he regarded her in silence, then abruptly turned and left.

"The Brant men really know how to rip a woman's heart apart," Samantha muttered to herself. It was now evening. Her duties for the day completed, she had escaped to the privacy of the back porch. Leaning back in the rocking chair, she frowned tiredly. Following breakfast, Johnny had tried a new tactic. Except for the time he was away with his father, he had spent the day trailing around after her and insisting on helping her with the chores. His behaviour was so exemplary it tore at her heart. And, he'd done all he could to make Melissa behave, too.

When their bedtime came, she'd given both of them tight hugs. "I will always remember the fun times we've had," she'd said, again making it clear that she could not remain as their housekeeper. Then she'd told both of them how much she loved them and assured them she would visit often.

Now she sat, her mind haunted by their wistful faces.

"Evening." Thatcher's voice broke into her thoughts.

She groaned inwardly. He'd seemed distracted all evening, and she'd been sure he wouldn't seek her out. But here he was. *He probably just has some instructions he wants to give me for tomorrow and then he'll leave,* she reasoned.

"Nice night," he said, leaning against the post he had leaned against the evening before.

"Yes," she replied, wishing he'd say what he'd come to say and then go back inside.

"The kids are very anxious to have you stay."

She glanced at him. This time there had been no accusation in his voice. He'd simply spoken as if stating a fact. "I'm sure they'll adapt quickly to whomever you hire. Probably a week after I'm gone they won't even notice my absence," she replied evenly.

"I doubt that." Hooking his thumbs in the pockets of his jeans, he said gruffly, "Truth is, I'm going to miss you, too."

Samantha's stomach knotted with anticipation. *Don't go getting your hopes up,* she cautioned herself. She'd had them dashed too many times before. "I've gotten used to having all of you around, too. It will be difficult for me to leave," she admitted.

For a moment he regarded her in silence, then said, "You're an attractive woman. I've always thought that. You're not exactly beautiful, but you can hold a man's attention."

"Thanks, I think," she replied, afraid to let herself speculate where this conversation was leading.

He shifted his shoulders uneasily. "But in the past, it always seemed as if we never could see eye to eye on anything. If I said something was black, you said it was white."

"That road went both ways," she said in her defense. "I can't remember when you ever agreed with me on anything without an argument."

A sheepishness came over his features. "You're right. For reasons I've never been able to figure out, I've always been intimidated by you."

Her eyes rounded in shock. "*You're* intimidated by me?"

He grinned self-consciously. "Maybe 'intimidated' is a bit too strong. You've always unnerved me. Guess that's why I've tended to overreact to everything you said or did."

"We've both sort of overreacted to each other," she said, recalling how nervous she'd always been when he was around.

He nodded, then the self-conscious grin faded and his expression became serious. "But since you've been here with us, I've gotten to know you and I've grown to enjoy your company."

Samantha's heart was beating wildly. "You're a lot easier to be around than I thought you would be," she managed in a surprisingly calm voice.

His smile returned. "I'm glad you think so." The smile vanished once again. Straightening, he faced her levelly. "This isn't easy for me."

How hard can it be to ask a woman out on a date? Samantha wondered. Then she recalled the guilt he felt about Laura's death. Fear that he would change his mind swept through her. *Say something encouraging,* she ordered herself. "I rarely bite." She flushed scarlet as what she had said registered in her brain. *Something a little more demure was what I had in mind,* she scolded herself, almost afraid to look at him. Half expecting to see him head for the door, she was surprised to see he didn't move.

"Glad to hear that," he replied with a hint of a nervous grin. Then his expression became more solemn than ever. "Like I said before, my children have gotten used to having you around and so have I. In fact, you've fit into our lives real well."

Samantha's heart slowed to a more normal rate as her hopes began to die. He'd brought up his children again. This didn't sound like a man getting ready to ask for a date. What it did sound like, she realized, was a man preparing to make a business proposal . . . one, she was fairly certain, his children had forced him into making. "If you're getting ready to ask me to stay on as your housekeeper, I can't," she said stiffly. "It really would cause too much gossip, and I do care about my reputation."

"I know." He shifted uneasily. "What I'm asking is if you'd be interested in staying on as my wife."

Samantha sat dumbfounded. She'd been hoping for a date. Instead, he'd asked her to marry him.

"Look, I know this has probably come as a shock to you. Truth is, I was a little surprised by the notion myself when it first struck me," he said, breaking the silence that had fallen between them. "You're nothing like Laura. She was easy to get along with. I figure you and I are going to have a few battles. But I've missed female companionship, and I can't deny I'm attracted to you. I can give you a decent life. I may not be the greatest husband in the world, but I'll do my best to please you."

She was shaken by how much she wanted to accept his offer. But she had to have some hope that one day he would allow himself to love her. "What about love?" she asked.

His expression hardened. "I've grown to like you and admire you. You would have my loyalty and friendship."

Hot tears burned at the back of her eyes. He'd asked her because he was sure their marriage would be a safe arrangement. Clearly he was certain he would never actually fall in love with her, and therefore his love for Laura would never be threatened. For one brief moment, the hope that maybe she could break down the barriers he kept around his heart blossomed, and she was tempted to accept his offer. Then reality returned. She forced herself to face the fact that all he would ever allow himself to feel for her was physical attraction. "I appreciate your offer, but I've sort of got my heart set on marrying someone who loves me," she managed to reply levelly.

He nodded his understanding. "Thought I might as well ask," he said. "Figured it couldn't do any harm."

Couldn't do any harm? she retorted silently. She felt as if she'd been ripped apart. She was hurting now, more than she had ever thought she could hurt. *The only way you're ever going to have any peace is to put a definite end to thoughts of a future with him,* she commanded herself. And it suddenly dawned on her how to do just that. "You're lucky I didn't take you up on your offer," she said stiffly. "There are things about me you would never be able to accept."

He raised a questioning eyebrow.

"I have druid ancestry. I see things in a crystal ball," she continued before she could lose her nerve. She'd expected him to laugh or to look shocked, then worried that she was crazy. But he did neither.

Instead he studied her narrowly. "You see things in a crystal ball?"

"It's an antique sphere that's been in our family for generations," she replied with a calmness she didn't feel. How could she have blurted out this secret? And to Thatcher Brant! *You did it because you wanted to rid yourself of the futile hope that the two of you could have a future together,* she reminded herself.

Great job! Any minute now he's going to shove you into his patrol car and take you to the state asylum. But again to her surprise, he treated her revelation with grim acceptance.

"What kind of things do you see?" he asked.

The intensity of his scrutiny set her nerves on an even sharper edge. "People. Images." She gave a nervous shrug. "Nothing earth-shattering."

He continued to regard her narrowly. "Do the other members of your family see these things?"

He's collecting data for when he carts me away to the asylum, she decided. *And he wants to know if he should worry about any of the rest of my family.* "No. I'm the only one," she replied.

He looked as if he didn't believe her. "What about your grandmother?"

She shook her head. "No. She never saw anything, either." Suddenly thinking of the gossip and whispering her revelation could cause if Thatcher did tell anyone else, she paled. Not only did she not want people talking about her, she didn't want her family to suffer. Knowing how some people exaggerated, pretty soon there would be insinuations that her entire family was crazy. "The truth is, my grandmother was the only one who even knew I saw anything in the crystal. My parents and sister don't know, and I'd appreciate it if you'd keep this between us."

For a long moment he regarded her without speaking, then said, "You can consider my lips sealed."

She drew a breath of relief. He'd given her his word he would keep her secret. "Thanks," she said gratefully.

He nodded, his expression remaining grim. Then abruptly he said, "Good night," and went inside.

Leaning back in the rocking chair, Samantha closed her eyes and issued a groan. It had been desperation that had caused her to reveal her secret to him. Now she felt like a complete idiot. "He'll probably have a new housekeeper hired by noon tomorrow and come up with some reason why I shouldn't stay another day," she murmured, still surprised he hadn't strapped her into a straitjacket and carted her off.

Chapter Nine

The next morning, Thatcher gave no indication that he and Samantha had even had a conversation the night before. During breakfast, he was guarded as usual but he didn't cast any glances her way that suggested he thought she was unstable and might go berserk at any moment.

Maybe he's just humoring me until he can find some way of easing me quickly out of his home, she decided. And she really couldn't blame him. If their positions had been reversed, she would have wondered about *his* sanity.

But the morning and afternoon passed like any other. Admittedly Thatcher was a bit more subdued than normal when he joined them for lunch, but he made no announcement about having found a new housekeeper. He'd also apparently kept his word about not revealing her secret, because Maude showed

no signs of uneasiness other than those associated with
the plans for the wedding.

*Thatcher's not the kind of man who makes snap
decisions. He likes to consider all the possibilities first,*
she reasoned as she put dinner on the table. He'd
probably been interviewing women all day and re-
viewing his impressions about those he'd already in-
terviewed. No doubt, during their evening meal, he
would inform them that he'd hired a new housekeeper, she concluded. But again he proved her wrong.

"I was so certain he'd want me out of here as soon
as possible," she murmured under her breath. Everyone had finished eating and now she stood alone in the
kitchen washing the pots and pans.

"Dinner was very good tonight."

She glanced over her shoulder to see Thatcher entering. *Here it comes,* she thought. A rush of relief
swept through her. All day she'd been waiting for the
other shoe to drop. Now it would. He was going to tell
her that he'd replaced her and that he wanted her
moved out of his house by noon tomorrow. She'd miss
the children, but this was for the best, she told herself. Aloud, she replied with a level, "Thanks," to the
compliment he'd just paid her.

"I was talking to Jack Faraday today," he said,
picking up a towel and beginning to dry the pots and
pans she had just washed.

Samantha's back stiffened. Jack Faraday was the
owner of the local drugstore and the town pharma-
cist. She suddenly found herself wondering if Thatcher
had gone to see the man in an attempt to find out if
she could be taking some kind of drug that would be
causing her to have hallucinations. Aloud she said
wryly, "I don't think he'd make a good housekeeper.

The fact that he stocks up on TV dinners has me convinced he can't cook. Besides, managing his store takes up most of his time.''

Thatcher grinned crookedly at her jest. "You're right. I'll take him off the list.''

Samantha forced a smile as her nerves grew more tense.

"The truth is, I went to see him about you,'' Thatcher said, his tone becoming businesslike.

Samantha felt a flush building. If he had confided in Jack about her claim of seeing images in a crystal ball, she would be totally humiliated. "What about me?'' she demanded.

He set aside the pan he'd been drying and looked at her. "I heard Nancy was retiring, which means Jack's going to be looking for someone to help him around the store. I told him you might be interested, and he said he thought you'd be terrific for the job. You wouldn't have to start for a few weeks, so you could stay on with us until the wedding the way we planned.''

Samantha stared at him in confusion. "You went out and found me a job here in Smytheshire for when I finish this one?''

"Smytheshire is your home,'' he said with authority. His jaw tensed. "I hope you'll at least consider Jack's offer. Boston's not a safe town for a woman alone.'' Having made this pronouncement, he put down the towel and left.

Samantha stared down at the dishwater. Thatcher's behavior made no sense at all. His order that she not carry her grandmother's Ouija board across his threshold had been so firm she'd been surprised he hadn't insisted she burn it or, at the very least, lock it away before he even allowed her into his home. But he seemed completely accepting about her admission to having seen images in a crystal ball.

By the time Maude and the children were settled for the night, her nerves were near the breaking point. "I can't stand this. I have to know why he's behaving so out of character," she muttered under her breath as she went back downstairs. She found him in the den putting away the toys he and the children had been playing with earlier.

"Did you get Maude settled for the night?" he asked as she entered.

"She's in bed reading," she replied. Her shoulders straightened with resolve. "Thatcher, there's something I have to know."

He'd just finished putting the pieces of a game back into their box. Closing it, he rose and faced her. "What do you want to know?"

"I have to know why I'm still here after what I told you last night," she said bluntly.

He drew a resigned breath. "You're here because I decided that it was impossible to fight the inevitable. It's time for me to stop overreacting to what I learned when Devin Smythe died and face the facts about this town and its residents."

Samantha frowned in confusion. "That sounds rather ominous."

"I didn't mean to sound quite so foreboding," he said in a milder voice. "And what I learned did explain a few things that had been bothering me—such as how Thelma Johnson knew her son had been injured from a fall out of a tree and that he was lying in the woods with a broken ankle when she was in town baking pies with a bunch of women at the church. Or how Sarah Delanney knew her father had had a heart attack and needed help out by the old mill. Or how Jerry Fields always knew just the right pitch to throw to strike me out when we played baseball in high school.''

"He knew the right pitch because you were always a sucker for a high, outside fastball," she interjected.

The hint of a smile curled one corner of his mouth. "Guess I was." Then his gaze narrowed. "But I'm surprised you remember that. I was under the impression there was nothing about me you found the least bit memorable."

How much she remembered about him would really shock him, she thought. She was somewhat shaken herself. "We were talking about inevitabilities and what you learned when Devin Smythe died," she reminded him, not wanting this conversation to take a turn that could embarrass her. He could never love her, and she wasn't going to be led into an admission of how strongly she felt toward him.

"Yeah." He frowned contemplatively. "It seems that a large percentage of our residents have druid blood running through their veins. However, I was led to believe that almost none of them know this."

"I've never heard anyone but my grandmother mention it," she responded to the question in his voice. "And when she told me, I had the impression she thought our heritage was unique to our family. I also know that she never told my mother or my sister. She had told my father a long time ago. According to her, he wasn't pleased or impressed. It's my guess he's either forgotten or will never repeat what she told him. And you're the only one I've ever told."

"Well, if there are others who do know about their heritage, they aren't spreading it around," Thatcher said. He shrugged. "I guess all towns have their secrets. They just don't have such a large collective one. But as far as I can tell, we're a pretty normal lot. It's just that a few of us have a little quirk of some kind or another."

Samantha studied him more closely as a sudden thought entered her mind. "And what about you? Do you have a little quirk of some kind or another?"

He scowled. "According to Zebulon, my ancestors knew his ancestors. But I haven't experienced any supernatural repercussions due to my lineage."

"Then when I told you about my seeing the images in the crystal, you believed me," Samantha said, marveling at this turn of events.

Thatcher raised an eyebrow. "I'm willing to buy a little ESP, even some telepathy between people under certain circumstances, but I'm not ready to believe in images in a crystal ball. What I believe is that you have an incredibly fertile imagination and that you spent too much time in your grandmother's company."

"How generous of you," she replied dryly.

For a long moment, Thatcher regarded her in a curt silence. Then a challenge flickered in his eyes. "All right. Let's go take a look at this crystal ball of yours."

Samantha wasn't certain why, but she balked at the thought of looking into the crystal with Thatcher nearby. "It won't do any good," she argued. "You won't see anything."

"Let's just say that I'm interested in seeing a druid antiquity," he countered.

"We can't leave the children and Maude unattended," she returned.

Thatcher started toward the door. "I'll tell Maude where we're going. If we're needed, she can phone us and we can be back here in less than a minute."

Stepping aside to allow him to pass, Samantha knew there was no way out of this. *He's always been as hardheaded as a mule,* she thought. *Besides, what difference would it make to show him the crystal? He won't see anything.*

Hearing him come down the stairs, she went out into the hall to meet him. After she retrieved her keys from her purse, they went next door. As they entered the living room and walked toward the crystal, Samantha noticed that it seemed to acquire a deep purplish tint. It's hues had always been faint before. *It must be reacting to Thatcher,* she decided, then was startled by this thought. She'd never considered the possibility of the crystal reacting to a person; it never had before. *I'm just overly tense,* she reasoned. It was probably just a reflection of something on the table making the crystal's hue look darker than normal. But when she scanned the contents of the table, there was nothing pink or purple.

"So that's your crystal ball," Thatcher said as they came to a halt beside the table.

He studied it skeptically. The hint of a smile began to play at one corner of his mouth. "Can I touch it?"

She scowled at him impatiently. "Of course you can touch it."

"Just thought I should ask," he said, his smile growing. "Mrs. Elberly won't let me near her crystals."

Samantha noticed that as Thatcher lifted the crystal from its base and held it cradled in his hand, the purple hue intensified. "It's very pretty," he said, the smile disappearing as he studied the sphere more intently.

Samantha's breath caught as a sudden burst of pink flashed from somewhere near the center of the crystal. The thought that the crystal was reacting to Thatcher's flattery flashed through her mind. *I'm loosing my grip on reality,* she berated herself frantically as the pink mingled with the purple like a lazy summer sunset.

"It's interesting the way it seems to change colors when it's placed in different positions," he said contemplatively.

Surely the crystal was merely picking up the colors of various objects in the room and reflecting them in its own way, she reasoned. Then another explanation occurred to her. Maybe it was reacting to Thatcher like one of those "mood" rings from the sixties. Something he had said a few moments ago came to mind. "Why won't Mrs. Elberly let you near her crystals?" she asked.

He grinned sheepishly. "She claims they sing very softly to her. But she says that when I get near them, they make a sound like cymbals clashing and it hurts her ears." He shook his head. "I think she needs her hearing aid adjusted."

Samantha drew a shaky breath. She'd heard Mrs. Elberly's crystals. When she was a young girl, her grandmother had taken her along on a couple of visits to the woman's house. Samantha had been fascinated by the crystalline formations, and when she'd stood very close, she'd been sure she'd heard them chime very, very softly. "They like you," Mrs. Elberly had told her.

Watching her own crystal's reaction to Thatcher, she heard herself saying, "Maybe you frighten them or they're afraid you won't like them."

He glanced at her and frowned as if suddenly he was worried about her.

That did sound crazy, she admitted, flushing with embarrassment. She was attributing emotions to inanimate objects. As if what she'd just said had been merely a jest, she gave a shrug and added with a dry laugh, "Or maybe Mrs. Elberly just doesn't want you getting near them because she's afraid you might pick one of them up and accidentally drop it. She's very protective of them."

"Maybe," he replied, his expression relaxing and his attention returning to the sphere. Setting it back in its holder, he glanced toward her challengingly. "Do you see anything in it right now?"

She peered down. The purple hue had subsided. Inside was Thatcher's image. She was there also. He was reaching out to her with a longing look on his face. Her heart began to beat harder, faster. Then Laura's image began to take form in front of Thatcher. His arms fell to his sides and he backed away. "I don't see anything," she lied, unable to bear hearing him again proclaim his allegiance to Laura.

When he made no response, she glanced toward him. He was scowling at the crystal, an expression of intense concentration on his face. "Do you see something?" she asked.

He gave a shrug. "Only your reflection," he replied curtly. Then glancing at his watch, he added coolly, "We'd better be getting home. It's late, and we have to be up early."

He looked irritated and she guessed he was berating himself for even showing an interest in what he believed to be utter nonsense. She glanced back at the crystal as he started toward the door. The purplish tint now had red highlights. She thought of Mrs. Elberly's crystals. Painfully loud, clashing cymbals seemed like a perfectly reasonable response to Thatcher, she mused as she followed him, turning off the lights as she went.

During the next few days Thatcher made no move to seek her out for any private conversations. *Guess the crystal ball was a little too much for him,* she decided, ripping weeds out of the flower garden lining the back porch. Dinner was over, but this time of year the sun remained out later. Thatcher was playing ball with the children toward the back of the yard. Howard and Maude were sitting in the front-porch swing enjoying the pleasant evening breeze. But Samantha had been too tense to sit still and she didn't feel like being in Thatcher's company. So she'd chosen to weed, hoping to put the man out of her mind by concentrating on her task. But he was still there. Out of the corner of her eye she saw him laughing and wrestling with Johnny. Looking down at her hand, she realized she'd just pulled up a fledgling daisy, totally missing the weed beside it. Quickly she replanted the flower. *I'd better take a break before I do any real destruction,* she decided. Brushing a stream of perspiration from her cheek, she sat back on the grass. As she drew her knees up and wrapped her arms around her jean-clad legs, she heard Thatcher's laughter mingled with that of the children. It was a deep resonant sound. She'd sat so she would not see him, but unable to resist, she looked over her shoulder toward him and the children. A sharp jab of pain seemed to pierce her heart. She wanted so much to have him look at her with the love he showed Melissa and Johnny. *That's never going to happen,* she told herself for the hundredth time. She forced her gaze back to the garden.

Suddenly a cry split the air. Turning back toward the children, she saw that Johnny had fallen near the apple tree. She was on her feet in an instant. By the time she reached the little boy, Thatcher was lifting him, and she could see blood running freely from a deep cut in Johnny's chin.

"He fell on an piece of exposed root," Thatcher said, his voice gruff with concern.

Melissa started crying at the sight of all the blood soaking both her father's and her brother's shirts.

"What happened?" Howard demanded, coming hurriedly around the house.

"I'll get a cloth from the kitchen," Samantha said, already running toward the house.

Thatcher followed, carrying the boy. "He fell," he told Howard as the older man picked up the sobbing Melissa and followed Thatcher.

"Your brother's going to be fine," Thatcher assured his daughter over his shoulder as they all entered the kitchen, but Melissa didn't look convinced and continued to cry softly.

Samantha had gotten out a clean dish towel. She pressed it tightly against the wound for a long moment, then slowly lifted it away and took a closer look. She saw Thatcher pale as he looked, too. "It's going to need stitches," he said, and she nodded.

Barely five minutes later, Samantha was sitting in the car with Johnny in her arms, holding a heavy folded cloth tightly against the boy's chin to stop the bleeding. She'd called Dr. Prescott, and he'd instructed her to bring Johnny to his office. She noticed Thatcher's hands shaking as he buckled her and Johnny in with the same set of seat belts.

"He's going to be all right," she said with calm confidence as Thatcher climbed in on the driver's side.

He nodded as if he knew this, too, but his expression remained grim.

Samantha forced a smile as she turned and waved to Maude, Howard and Melissa, who were all watching from the porch. At least Melissa had stopped crying, she thought thankfully. Although the little girl still looked upset, she seemed reassured that her brother would be fine.

Samantha glanced at Thatcher as they pulled out onto the street. The paleness of his complexion shook her, but his voice carried conviction as he spoke comfortingly to his son.

"Seems my family is keeping Dr. Prescott busy these days," he said, attempting some light bantering.

"So it would seem," she replied, gently combing Johnny's hair away from his face. The child was lying silently against her and she studied him worriedly, wondering if he might be going into shock. Thank goodness they were only a couple of minutes from the doctor's place, she thought.

Thatcher glanced toward the boy. "Son?" he said sharply, clearly worried about shock, also.

The boy blinked.

"He's going to be fine," Samantha said, forcing a calmness into her voice she didn't feel. "You concentrate on your driving," she ordered Thatcher as the car drifted over the center line.

Thatcher grimaced and jerked his attention back to the road.

A couple of minutes later they pulled into the doctor's drive. Reid Prescott came out to meet them.

The next half hour was the most harrowing Samantha ever recalled having gone through. She and Thatcher helped the doctor hold Johnny still while he gave him a shot and then stitched the chin. Feeling mildly nauseous, Samantha looked away from the doctor's hands as he sewed the torn skin. Her gaze fell on Thatcher. He was watching the doctor work. The color had drained totally from his face and her concern shifted from Johnny to his father.

She leaned toward Thatcher, bringing her mouth close to his ear. "Don't watch. It won't help if you pass out," she ordered in a hushed voice so that Johnny couldn't hear.

Thatcher drew a shaky breath, nodded and looked at her. The anguish she saw in his eyes tore at her. "The doctor will patch him up good as new," she said softly, and the answering gratitude in his gaze caused her heart to skip a beat.

At last Johnny's chin was stitched. The doctor gave them some pain pills for when the shot he'd given Johnny wore off and a prescription for some antibiotics the boy was to take for the next few days.

"Let's get him home first. You put him to bed and I'll go to the drugstore," she instructed Thatcher as they left Dr. Prescott's office and walked toward the car.

Thatcher nodded as she slipped into her seat and he placed Johnny on her lap. "Thanks for being here," he said, touching her cheek with a light caress. Then, after gently mussing his son's hair, he closed the door, walked around the car and climbed in.

A little later, as Samantha drove to the drugstore, she noticed that her hands were shaking. Parenthood was a very scary proposition at times. But it was worth it, she admitted, recalling how warm and fulfilled she had felt when she'd looked down at Johnny during the ride home from the doctor's and seen him looking up at her with love and gratitude in his eyes. She'd hugged him and he'd grinned. Tears welled in her eyes. The desire to have a family of her own grew stronger.

With a frustrating persistence, Thatcher's image again filled her mind. She already loved his children as if they were her own. But Thatcher lacked the most important qualification for the husband she wanted. "I need a man who loves me," she said aloud, refusing to give in to the weakness she had for Thatcher. Her chin firmed with determination. "And I'll find one."

Chapter Ten

Samantha rolled over in bed and looked at the clock. It was a little after two in the morning. She'd had a dream about Johnny's accident, and it had woken her. "Go back to sleep," she ordered under her breath. But her eyes remained open while Johnny's tearful face filled her mind. Giving in to the inevitable, she rose, pulled on her robe and went to check on the boy. He was sleeping peacefully.

Thirsty, she went downstairs to the kitchen for a drink of water.

"I wanted to thank you again for all you did for Johnny and me this evening."

Samantha nearly dropped the glass she was filling. Her thirst forgotten, she set it aside and turned to face Thatcher as he entered from the back porch. He was dressed only in a pair of worn jeans. His hair was mussed and tired lines were etched into his face. "You startled me," she said, still badly shaken by his unexpected appearance. "I thought you went to bed ages ago."

He shrugged. "Couldn't sleep."

She regarded him worriedly. "You look exhausted."

"I am," he admitted, "but every time I close my eyes, I see Johnny with all that blood on his face."

"Kids get hurt. That's part of growing up," she replied soothingly.

He nodded as he approached her. Gently he combed a wayward strand of hair from her cheek, tucking it behind her ear. "I think I would have blacked out in the doctor's office today if you hadn't ordered me to look away," he said.

His finger left a trail of fire. She ordered herself to ignore it. "You did have me worried for a moment," she confessed.

He raked a hand through his hair. "It's a shame you can't stay on as our housekeeper. We make a good team."

There was a hint of little-boy helplessness behind the frustration on his face. It made her want to try to work out some arrangement that would allow her to stay. *Don't be a fool,* she chided herself. "That would be impossible," she said aloud, as much for herself as for him.

"Yeah, I know," he replied.

Samantha swallowed hard. He looked like he needed a comforting hug and she wanted to give him one. That could be really dangerous, her inner voice warned. She dropped her gaze from his face. Immediately she knew she'd made a big mistake. As her eyes focused on his hair-matted chest, embers deep within

her began to glow with the warmth of womanly longing.

"I would feel safe leaving my children in your
care," he was saying with regret. "I could go off to
work and not worry about them."

"I'm sure you can find someone just as reliable as
me," she managed, marveling that she had been able
to put together a coherent sentence.

He cupped her face and tilted it upward. "But will
I be able to find someone who cares as much about
them as you do?" he demanded gruffly. "It was obvious how much Johnny's suffering affected you."

His touch made thinking close to impossible. As his
thumb ran along the line of her jaw, the glowing embers became a roaring blaze. "I should be going back
upstairs now," she said, but her legs refused to move,
and the brown of his eyes darkened.

"You look so deliciously appetizing," he murmured, his fingers twining into her hair.

Her tongue came out to wet her suddenly dry lips.

"You've always been destructive to my peace of
mind," he growled. "I've fought admitting it even to
myself, but you arouse the lust in me more strongly
than any woman ever has. You always have."

Her breath locked in her lungs as his mouth found
hers. He kissed her lightly at first, small nibbling
kisses.

She told herself to pull free, but still her legs refused to respond.

As he claimed her mouth fully, she surrendered to
the longing within her. Her hands moved over his hair-
roughened chest. The firm texture of his body beneath her palms sent thrills of excitement coursing
through her.

When his arms circled her, drawing her up against his length, she reveled at the feel of the hard columns of his legs pressing against hers.

Trembles of delight shook her as she ran her hands over his shoulders, then along the strong cords of his neck. As her fingers entwined in his hair, she wanted to cry out with sheer ecstasy.

Thatcher issued a moan of pleasure as he deepened the kiss and pulled her even closer.

That he wanted her was evident, and her own body craved to surrender to his desire.

Then slowly, he lightened the kiss and let his hold on her relax. But he did not release her entirely. Instead, he kept his arms around her and his hands pressed lightly on her back.

"It would seem," he said, continuing to drop light kisses on her lips, "that the physical attraction I feel toward you is mutual."

"It would be a little silly for me to deny it," she replied, the tantalizing feel of his warm breath adding more fuel to the fire now raging within her.

"Marry me," he ordered huskily.

Agreement was on the tip of her tongue. "I have to know there's a chance you could learn to love me," she heard herself saying. Realizing how close this was to a confession of how deep her feelings for him had grown, her body tensed.

He stopped kissing her and for a long moment stood frozen. Then slowly he released her and she felt his barrier rebuilding itself. "I can't make that promise," he said as he took a step back away from her. "What I can promise is loyalty and fidelity."

She wanted desperately to be in his arms again, to feel his warmth enveloping her. As if they had a will of their own, her hands began to reach out toward him. Abruptly she balled them into fists and forced them to her sides. "That's not enough," she said.

He was studying her now in a guarded silence. "It's all I can offer."

"I know," she replied. She told herself to go back up to bed before she made an even bigger fool of herself, but she'd been keeping too much bottled up for too long. "I can't believe the situation I've gotten myself into," she said with self-directed anger. "I've fallen in love with you." Her cheeks paled as she realized she'd just blurted out this confession. *Well, he had to have guessed by now, anyway,* she reasoned. She forced herself to meet his gaze squarely. He looked uncomfortable, as if he was trying to think of something to say but couldn't.

Unable to stand still, she began to pace. Coming to a halt near the stove, she turned to face him again. "Who would ever believe it?" She shoved a hand into her hair. "I can hardly believe it myself. Me and Thatcher Brant. All my instincts warned me to stay away from you, but even in my wildest flights of fancy it never occurred to me that this could be a consequence of disobeying those instincts."

Thatcher started toward her, his expression one of purpose. "I would be a good husband to you."

She knew if he started kissing her again, she might allow him to convince her of that. "Don't get near me," she warned, rounding the table to keep it between them.

He placed his palms flat on the table and leaned toward her. "Most marriages have a few problems. People work through them. I'll be your friend. I'll stand by you. I'll never be a wealthy man, but I'll keep food on our table and a roof over our heads."

Tears of frustration burned at the back of her eyes. "You will never know how much I want to take you up on that offer," she said. "But I know my limitations. I understand your feelings toward Laura and I respect them. I would never expect you to forget her or stop loving her. But I need you to love me, too. I would need to know that it's me you're making love to in our bed, not her."

His gaze narrowed. "I'd know which woman I was with."

Challenge flickered in her eyes. "But you'd be wishing I was Laura." The frustration she was feeling entered her voice. "You keep her memory so alive, so strong, I sometimes think I should be setting a place for her at the table. You're a good man, Thatcher Brant, and I'd like to be married to you, but I can't live my life in another woman's shadow."

A haunted look came into his eyes. "I owe Laura. She died for me. I can't betray her."

The resolve in his eyes was enough to convince Samantha that his mind would never be changed, still, she couldn't stop herself from trying. "Laura was an adult. She made a decision to have a child. It was her decision, not yours."

His jaw hardened. "She did it for me."

The pain in his voice tore at Samantha. "You're taking too much responsibility for another person's actions," she said tiredly, knowing her words were futile but needing to say them, anyway. "I hope for your sake that one day you'll forgive yourself." Unable to face him any longer, she left the kitchen.

Tears of regret trickled down her cheeks as she climbed the stairs and entered her room. Not wanting to wake Maude, she kept as silent as possible as she climbed back into bed. *I can just picture the shock on the faces of the citizens of Smytheshire if they knew I was crying over Thatcher Brant,* she thought, trying to stop the flow by finding some humor in her situation. But, the silent tears continued to stream from her eyes.

The sound of a stair creaking let her know that Thatcher was on his way to his room. She heard his light footfalls as he padded barefoot down the hall. Unexpectedly, the footsteps stopped at the door of her room.

Her heart began to beat faster. Had he decided that what she said made sense? Would he come in and tell her there was a chance for them? She felt dizzy and realized she was holding her breath.

Then the footsteps resumed. Thatcher entered Johnny's room for a moment, then she heard him going on down the hall to his own room.

Silly fool! she berated herself. Even if Thatcher did decide to forgive himself, he wouldn't come looking for her. He'd asked her to marry him because she was safe, because she wasn't a threat. He would never fall in love with her.

A groan escaped Samantha's lips as the alarm on the bedside table woke her. Reaching over, she turned it off, then covered her head with her pillow. Beneath the fluffy covering, she issued another groan. She'd actually confessed to Thatcher that she was in love with him.

"Are you ill?" Maude asked worriedly from her bed.

Come on, you have to face the day, Samantha ordered herself. "No, I'm fine," she replied, tossing off the pillow and forcing herself to get up.

"You look terrible," Maude persisted anxiously as Samantha dressed. "Are you sure you're not coming down with the flu?"

"I'm sure," Samantha said, applying a little makeup in hope of covering the ravages of the night. Knowing Maude would keep questioning her until she gave some sort of explanation for the circles under her eyes, she added, "Johnny's accident shook me up and I didn't sleep well."

"Boys are always doing crazy stunts and needing stitches," Maude said knowingly. "Thatcher certainly did his share."

Before Maude could launch into a story about Thatcher's youth, Samantha said she had to go get the coffee started and escaped. She wanted to put the man out of her mind, not listen to tales of his youthful escapades.

Reaching the kitchen, she discovered Thatcher already there starting the pot of coffee. He didn't look as if he'd gotten much sleep, either. "I stopped by Johnny's room," she said. "He requested pancakes for breakfast."

"It appears he's gotten over the trauma of getting stitches," Thatcher responded. His tone and manner businesslike, he glanced toward the calendar on the wall. "Looks like the date of Mom's wedding is getting close. Guess I'd better find that new housekeeper soon."

He was letting her know that there would be no more talk about *their* getting married. She told herself she should be relieved. Instead a hard knot formed in her stomach. Busying herself with gathering the ingredients for the pancakes, she said coolly, "Guess you'd better."

"Yeah," he returned as if he felt the need to confirm his intention. Then, heading for the door, he said, "I'll go see if Melissa is ready to get up."

And I hope he decides today on someone to hire, she added to herself.

But at neither lunch nor dinner did he mention having hired a new housekeeper.

"I was sure he'd not only find someone, but force Maude to allow the woman to immediately take my place," she muttered to herself as she sat on the back porch late that evening. He had, she did note, avoided her as much as possible.

The sound of the screen door opening caused her to glance around. It was Thatcher. His expression was coolly impersonal. *He's finally come to tell me who he's hired and enlist my aid in getting her into his home and me out of it as quickly as possible,* she thought. Her gaze traveled across the lawn to her own home. It might be lonely, but at least she wouldn't have Thatcher around to remind her of what a fool she'd made of herself last night.

"I've decided to hire Leona Boggs," he said, coming to a halt a couple of feet from her. "She did a good job raising her own children and she likes taking care of people. Johnny and Melissa have known her all their lives. They like her. And I'm sure we can survive her culinary experiments." Instead of leaning casually against a pillar as he normally did, he continued to stand rigidly. "If you'd like, I'll speak to Maude about allowing Leona to start work fairly soon. If I point out that it would be less of a change for the children if you and she didn't both leave at the same time, I'm sure she'll agree.''

Mentally Samantha patted herself on the back for being right. He couldn't wait to get rid of her. She'd miss the children and Maude, but she was as anxious to leave as he was to have her gone. "I do have a life I'd like to get back to," she replied.

Relief spread over his face. "Leona said she could start the day after tomorrow, if Maude was agreeable.''

"Sounds fine to me," Samantha replied, the enthusiasm in her voice genuine. If she could have moved out tonight, she would have.

Now that these arrangements were settled, she expected Thatcher to leave. Instead he regarded her indecisively for a long moment, then said, "I was in the drugstore today and happened to speak to Jack Faraday. He says you never contacted him about the job I mentioned to you.''

His show of concern about her future grated on her nerves. It felt too much like pity. He didn't want her and she didn't want him feeling responsible for her. Her shoulders squared with pride. "I didn't contact him because I have no intention of seeking that job. Like I told you before, I'm going to Boston.''

Disapproval flickered in his eyes. "Smytheshire is your home.''

"My home is wherever I choose!" she snapped back. She'd tried all day not to think about the fact that he could never love her. But now the thought filled her mind and it hurt. "You've got no say in my life. I'll make my own decisions about where I live.''

He glowered at her. "You've got to be the most obstinate woman on the face of this earth."

"And you've got to be the most thickheaded man," she retorted.

His jaw tensed. "Well, at least we're having a conversation that's more normal for the two of us than some we've had lately," he muttered. Then turning on his heel, he strode back into the house.

And so, as far as he's concerned, we're back to the way it was between us before I moved into his home, Samantha concluded. Becoming romantically involved with Thatcher was an absurd notion from the start. She promised herself, from this moment on, she would never contemplate such a ridiculous possibility again.

Chapter Eleven

Samantha set her suitcase down on her kitchen floor.
It was late afternoon. Leona had moved into Thatcher's house that morning. Samantha had remained
during the day to help her get acquainted with her
duties. But Thatcher would be returning home for
dinner soon, and she had wanted to be gone before he
arrived.

Saying goodbye to the children had been difficult.
They'd looked at her as if she was deserting them.
"Samantha's going to be right next door," Maude had
told them. That had cheered them up, and Samantha
hadn't had the heart to tell them she wouldn't be there
for long.

Standing alone in her kitchen, she looked around.
She'd always experienced a feeling of being warmly
greeted when she entered this room, but today that
feeling was missing. Instead, the room seemed empty

and uninviting. The sound of a car caught her attention, and she glanced out the window to see Thatcher pulling into his drive. Suddenly the desire to be where there was no possibility of seeing him was overwhelming.

Now is as good a time as any to begin searching for a job in Boston, she told herself. Of course, she'd have to come back for the surprise shower Julia Johnson was planning for Maude, and for the wedding itself. But she wasn't going to wait around Smytheshire in the meantime. She had to get her new life started. Reaching for the phone, she dialed Madaline Darnell's number in Boston.

Madaline greeted her with delight. "Samantha, I've been hoping you would call soon!" Curiosity laced her voice as she asked, "What's going on between you and Chief Brant?"

"Nothing," Samantha replied, surprised by the question.

"I find that a little hard to believe," Madaline returned skeptically. "First I hear that you've moved into his house to take care of his mother and children while Maude recovers from a broken leg. That in itself stunned me. I thought the two of you couldn't be in the same room together without having an argument. Then this morning Thatcher calls Colin to say that you're determined to come to Boston to work and asks if Colin and I would keep an eye on you."

"He didn't!" Samantha gasped, furious that Thatcher would interfere in her life. They'd both agreed that there was no place for her in his and she didn't want him in hers.

"Yes, he did," Madaline replied. "And Colin said he sounded honestly concerned. Anyway, you're to come stay with us when you come to town."

That Thatcher had appointed himself her guardian rankled Samantha. He was acting as if she were a kid sister who needed looking after. "I really can't impose like that," she said, adding apologetically, "And Thatcher had no right to ask."

"It's not an imposition," Madaline assured her. "I was going to ask you to stay with us, anyway. Now that Colin has given Thatcher his word, you're forced to. My husband takes his promises seriously." A coaxing quality entered her voice. "We'll have fun. You can fill me in on what's been happening in Smytheshire and I'll show you the sights of Boston."

Samantha felt trapped. To refuse would be impolite. Besides, she liked Madaline, and although she was still a little intimidated by Colin, she liked him, too. "If you're sure that's what you want," she conceded.

"I'm positive," Madaline responded happily. "Now when do you want to come?"

Samantha's gaze shifted to the window and Thatcher's house beyond. "As soon as possible."

"Today's Tuesday," Madaline said thoughtfully, "so come this Friday. I'll set up some interviews for you next week with people Colin and I know. In the meantime, I can get you acquainted with Boston."

"I'll be there," Samantha replied.

As she hung up the phone, the lonliness she'd experienced when she'd first entered her home again washed over her. Drawing a shaky breath, she picked up her suitcase and carried it upstairs to her room. Her mother had called earlier that day and invited her for dinner. At first Samantha had considered refusing. Her mother knew her better than anyone and could always sense when she was upset. And even though Sally Hogan was not the kind of mother who constantly interfered in her daughter's life, she could be persistent if she thought there was something going on that needed to be talked about. However, because Samantha needed to tell her parents about her plans to go to Boston, she had accepted the invitation.

"But I'm not ready to tell my mother about Thatcher," Samantha muttered as she unpacked. The truth was, she might never be ready to talk about Thatcher. "What I'm really hoping is that in a couple of weeks I'll have put him out of my mind and there won't be anything *to* talk about."

Dinner went more much smoothly than she'd expected. Her parents accepted her decision to go to Boston without protest. "Of course, we'd prefer for you to stay in Smytheshire," her father said, "but we understand your need to spread your wings."

Samantha was a bit surprised by their attitude. Later in the kitchen their reasoning became clear. "I can't help feeling that something is wrong," Molly said as she and Samantha washed the dishes.

"I'm just a little restless," Samantha replied.

"It's because of Johnny and Melissa." Sally smiled her motherly knowing smile. "You've always loved children and now you want a family of your own." She nodded as if confirming her words. "I'll admit I'm not thrilled with your decision to go to Boston, but your father and I realize that you're never going to find a husband in Smytheshire. No one here seems to suit you. And we do want you to find someone who will make you happy.''

Samantha drew a relieved breath. Her mother's explanation fitted the facts well, and Samantha could agree to it without feeling like a liar. It also saved her from any further probing. ''I'd like to find a man to share my life with,'' she admitted honestly.

Sally paused and gave her daughter a hug. ''And one day you will,'' she said with conviction. Returning to her dishes, she laughed lightly. ''I still can't believe you and Thatcher survived under the same roof for more than a month without a royal battle. Talk about two people totally unsuited for one another....''

Samantha forced a smile. ''Totally unsuited.''

Later, as she entered her house, she glanced toward Thatcher's place. Night had come, but in the light from the moon she saw him sitting in his usual spot on the front porch. I wish him happiness with his ghost, she thought tiredly.

Feeling a headache building, she went into the kitchen and took a couple of aspirin. She was exhausted but restless at the same time. Switching off the lights as she went, she began to make her way toward the stairs and her bed. But as she turned off the light in the living room, her restlessness grew. Going up to bed would be futile, she decided and instead sank down into the large overstuffed chair in front of the fireplace.

''Ouch!'' Samantha shifted into a more upright position and glanced at the illuminated dial on her watch. It was a little after one in the morning. She'd fallen asleep in the chair and now she had a crick in her neck.

And it was Thatcher's fault, she seethed. He was the reason she'd been too restless to go up to bed. "I've always associated him with a pain in the neck," she muttered. Then she frowned. She'd ordered herself to not think about him, but there he was—the very first thing she thought about when she awoke.

Furious with herself, she rubbed harder on the knot in her neck. Attempting to stretch it out, she sat up still straighter. It was then that the sound of a car pulling out onto the street registered in her mind. Going to the window, she saw that Thatcher's car was gone. His starting the engine must have been what woke her up, she realized.

Concern for him swept through her. "He's a big boy. He can take care of himself," she told herself curtly. Nevertheless, her uneasiness lingered.

As she forced her gaze away from the view beyond the window, a flicker of color caught her attention. There was a full moon tonight and the light it cast through the panes gave the crystal sphere a bluish glow. Like a moth to a flame, she moved toward it and peered into it.

In the dim light she saw a shadowy face. Her gaze not leaving the crystal, she reached over and switched on the nearby lamp. A gasp escaped as she recognized Luther Conley. He was smiling, a very evil, malicious smile.

The uneasiness she'd been feeling turned to fear. "Thatcher can take care of himself," she told herself again. But the fear remained strong. "I don't even know what seeing Luther's face in the crystal means," she muttered, debating what she should do or if she should even do anything.

Crossing the room, she reached for the phone. Maybe she should warn Thatcher. A dry smiled curled her lips. And just what was she going to tell him? That she'd seen Luther in the crystal? He thought the images she saw were merely due to vivid imagination.

Maybe he already knows Luther is back in town, she reasoned. *Maybe Luther is the reason he'd just left.* And there was always the possibility that Luther might come back and not cause any trouble. "However that doesn't seem very likely," she admitted, pacing around the room.

"I could call Mary just to make certain she's all right," she decided aloud, searching for something to do that would alleviate her growing anxiety. As she found Mary's phone number, though, and started to dial, she stopped. She was acting like her grandmother. The people in this town had come to dread Ada's early-morning calls. "She was only trying to be helpful, but people did hate to hear from her, and I know she probably ruined what would most likely have been perfectly good days for a lot of people by worrying them unnecessarily."

Her gaze shifted to her watch. It was nearly two. If Mary was having a peaceful night's sleep, she'd never forgive Samantha for waking her. "And I'd feel like a fool," Samantha added glumly.

The walls seemed to be closing in on her. "I could go for a drive past Mary's house," she said, already heading for the door.

As she pulled out onto the street, she scowled at her image in the rearview mirror. "Maybe I do need my head examined. First I fall in love with Thatcher Brant and now I'm out at two in the morning cruising the streets because I saw Luther Conley in my crystal ball.'' She grimaced. ''I sound like a lunatic.''

But she didn't turn back.

As she turned down Mary's street, her heart began to beat faster. Thatcher's car was there. The blinds on the windows in the living room were pulled down, but she could see light around the edges. ''Thatcher's probably got the situation under control,'' she assured herself as she continued past the house. However, it wouldn't hurt to check, she decided. At the intersection of Maple and Chestnut Streets, she turned the corner and parked on Maple.

I can't believe I'm doing this, she thought a few minutes later as she quietly made her way toward one of Mary's living-room windows. *I'm going to get arrested as a Peeping Tom,* she added, feeling more foolish by the second. A thorn from one of the rose-bushes in the garden beneath the window scratched her hand. She gulped back the startled cry of pain that threatened to escape. Rising on tiptoe, she peered through the tiny crack on the side of the blind. Lace curtains obscured the view, but she could discern Mary standing in the middle of the room. Then she saw a man walk up to her. *It was Luther.* He struck Mary and she fell back, knocking over a table on her way to the floor. Samantha's stomach knotted in fear. *Where was Thatcher?*

As if in answer, she heard his voice. ''Leave her alone, Luther,'' he ordered.

Luther laughed. ''You're in no position to be telling me what to do, Brant.''

Samantha shifted to the other side of the window and peered in. She saw Thatcher seated in a straight-back chair. His arms were pulled back in a manner that suggested his hands were tied behind him. An ugly bruise was developing along one side of his face.

"What are you going to do?" Mary asked as she got painfully to her feet.

Luther grinned at her. "I'm going to take the chief here for a ride. And tomorrow morning, bright and early, you're going to go by the bank and take out that little nest egg of yours. Then you come back here. I'll call and let you know where to bring the money. If you're a good girl and do as I say, you can save Chief Brant's life."

"He's going to kill me, anyway, and he'll kill you, too," Thatcher warned her.

"Now, Chief, you mustn't be so pessimistic," Luther chided. He turned toward Mary again. "You'll do as I say, right?"

"I'll do it," she promised. "Just don't hurt the chief."

"He's my ace in the hole," Luther assured her. "I'll take good care of him."

"Don't listen to him, Mary," Thatcher warned grimly.

Luther glowered at him. "You're trying my patience, Brant. If you keep it up, I'll forget about the money and simply shoot the two of you."

Samantha saw Thatcher's jaw twitch in anger but he clamped his mouth shut. She knew he was right. Luther was going to kill them. Frantically she tried to think of a way to help. She could use the radio in Thatcher's car to call Dan, Thatcher's deputy. He was on duty at the jail. But that would take time she didn't think she had.

As proof she was right, she heard Luther ordering Thatcher to his feet. "Now you just walk out that front door and to your car. Don't make any trouble and you won't get hurt," Luther instructed.

Watching, Samantha saw that Thatcher's hands were being held behind him with a pair of handcuffs.

"Remember, you promised you wouldn't hurt him," Mary said, her voice pleading.

"I remember, I remember," Luther replied amicably. "You just remember to get that money."

"I will," she promised again.

Samantha made her way toward the porch steps. She wasn't sure what she was going to do, but she knew she had to do something. Every instinct warned her that Luther was lying and that if Thatcher wasn't freed now he would be dead within the hour.

Searching for a way to help, she watched Thatcher walking down the steps. He was moving slowly. There was a tenseness about him that let her know he was preparing to attempt an escape. *He'll need a little help,* she told herself. She crouched low in the shadows.

As Luther reached the sidewalk, she lunged at him pushing him to the ground. She'd hoped he would drop the gun, but he didn't. Acting swiftly, Thatcher swung around, kicking at the hand that held the weapon. But Luther was too fast. He managed to jerk out of the way. Lying back, he aimed the gun at Thatcher and laughed. "Killing you is going to be a pleasure," he said, his finger tightening on the trigger.

Suddenly an anguished cry split the night air. Samantha saw the flash of metal as Mary swung an iron poker, striking Luther on the head. "You've hurt enough people!" the woman sobbed, hitting him again.

"Mary, stop!" Samantha and Thatcher cried out in unison as the woman raised the poker to deliver a third blow.

Mary froze in midmotion. Weeping hysterically, she dropped the poker. Sinking down onto the grass, she buried her face in her hands.

"Get the keys for these cuffs out of Luther's pocket," Thatcher ordered Samantha.

She looked down at Luther's lifeless body, his sightless eyes open staring at the night sky. Swallowing back a sudden threat of nausea, she obeyed.

"What the devil are you doing here?" Thatcher demanded harshly as she freed him.

She faced him levelly. "I saw Luther in my crystal ball."

"You could have gotten yourself killed," he growled.

"If I had, it would have been by *my choice*. The same way it's *your choice* to risk your life every day for the citizens of Smytheshire," she snapped back.

For a long moment he glowered at her in silence. Finally he said, "You've got a real bullheaded streak in you when it comes to making a point."

"And you're just plain bullheaded," she shot back, her frustration surfacing again.

"Guess I am," he admitted. His gaze swung to Mary. "I'll call her parents. You drive her out to their place. I'll have Dr. James or Dr. Prescott meet you there. She's going to need a sedative.''

Samantha nodded and turned her attention to Mary.

The woman obeyed without protest as Samantha helped her to her feet. But as Samantha started to guide her down the walk, Mary suddenly stopped and turned back to Thatcher. ''I'm so sorry, Chief,'' she said through her tears. ''He made me call you.''

Approaching her, Thatcher touched her shoulder gently. ''It's all right, Mary. It's over. You saved my life.''

''He was a truly evil man,'' she said.

''You go on to your parents' place now,'' he ordered softly but firmly.

''Come on,'' Samantha urged, again guiding the woman to her car.

As they made their way around the corner of the block, Mary stopped crying. She was stoically silent while Samantha helped her into the passenger seat. But as Samantha slid in behind the wheel, the woman began to speak in a monotone. ''Luther said if I didn't call the chief and get him to come over to my place, he'd take me down to the jail and make me watch him kill Dan,'' she said. ''I knew he meant it. He told me he'd killed a man in prison. He bragged about how he'd made it look like self-defense. I could tell he'd enjoyed the killing.''

Mary fell silent again and Samantha glanced at her worriedly. She was pale and her face was expressionless.

"So I called the chief and told him what Luther told me to tell him," Mary began to speak again as if compelled by a need to recite the events of the night. "I said that Luther had been to my home, taken what valuables he could find and then left. I said I was scared and that I wanted to go out to my parents' place, but Luther had taken my car. I said I knew Dan was on duty, but that Luther had hit me and I didn't want Dan to see me. Chief Brant's a goodhearted man. He came right away."

"Yes, he is a good man," Samantha agreed.

A tear began to trickle down Mary's cheek. "Luther promised me that he wouldn't harm the chief. He said he just wanted a hostage. But down deep I knew he was lying. He blamed Chief Brant and me for sending him to prison. Luther believed in exacting revenge. I'd made up my mind to warn the chief. I was going to yell out to him when he started up the walk. But Luther must have suspected. He tied me up and gagged me. Then he opened the front door and stood behind it. When the chief came in looking for me, Luther hit him. The blow stunned the chief long enough for Luther to get the chief's gun."

Mary's tears dried up again. For the first time, she looked at Samantha. "I know it's not right to kill anyone, but I couldn't let Luther leave with the chief."

Releasing one hand from the steering wheel, Samantha gave Mary's hand a squeeze. "You saved Thatcher's life and probably mine, as well. Thank you."

Mary drew a shaky breath. "When I married Luther, I thought he was a gentle kind man."

"People can surprise us," Samantha said quietly, thinking of Thatcher.

"At least Luther won't be surprising anyone anymore," Mary replied quietly.

Chapter Twelve

Samantha opened one eye. Light was streaming in through the window. Lifting her head, she opened the other eye and focused her gaze on the clock on the bedside table. It was nearly noon. "Well, I didn't get to bed until after five this morning," she reminded herself.

After she'd taken Mary to her parents' place, she told herself to go home. Instead, she'd gone searching for Thatcher. He and Dr. James were still at Mary's house.

Using the pretext of wanting to let Thatcher know she'd gotten Mary safely to her parents', Samantha managed to check on him and assure herself that the blow he'd received hadn't done any serious damage. Then she'd gone home.

Closing her eyes, she saw Thatcher's face as he'd looked last night. The bruise developing along one side had added a further grimness to his haggard appearance.

"Maybe you should consider hiring Samantha as a deputy the next time there's an opening," Dr. James had suggested with a grin when she'd joined the two men.

"She is a good woman to have by a man's side," Thatcher had conceded.

"As long as there's no emotional commitment involved," Samantha muttered now, opening her eyes to rid Thatcher's image from her mind. "You've got to stop thinking about him and concentrate on your preparations for Boston," she ordered herself as she tossed off her covers, rose and dressed.

But as she passed the living room on her way to the kitchen, she stopped in her tracks. She blinked once, thinking she must be seeing things. Then she scowled. She wasn't hallucinating. Thatcher was seated in her overstuffed chair, sleeping. How was she going to put him out of her mind when he wouldn't stay out of her life? she seethed silently.

Her scowl deepened as she wondered how he'd gotten in. Then she remembered that Maude had a key to her house. She'd given it to her when Maude was helping with Grandma Ada.

Her chin trembled at the sight of the bruise on Thatcher's face. It was larger than it had been a few hours ago. The knowledge of how close he'd come to getting himself killed caused a shiver of fear. The desire to remain in Smytheshire to keep an eye on him and try to protect him was strong. *He's a big boy. He can take care of himself,* she told herself, furious with this weakness. Her jaw firmed with resolve. She deserved to have a life of her own.

Pulling her gaze away from him, Samantha continued into the kitchen. She had just finished filling the percolator and plugging it in when she heard booted steps coming down the hall. As they reached the kitchen she steeled herself. "Isn't there a law against entering people's houses uninvited?" she said stiffly, turning to face Thatcher.

"I didn't want to take a chance on your leaving for Boston before I could talk to you," he replied, coming to a halt about three feet from her.

He was studying her with that guarded look she'd grown so used to seeing. *He's not going to change my mind about leaving,* she promised herself. Aloud she said, "I was under the impression we'd said all there was to say."

His eyes darkened with purpose. "No, we haven't." He took another step toward her. "I missed you last evening. I've gotten used to having you around. The kids missed you, too."

His words tore at her heart. *He'll never love you,* her inner voice screamed. "Thatcher, don't do this to me," she pleaded angrily. "You're not being fair."

"What I haven't been is honest," he replied. "Last night when I got home from work and you weren't there, I wanted to come over here and bring you back. I couldn't stop thinking about you ... wondering how you were spending your evening."

A haunted look came into his eyes. "I ordered myself to forget you. But when I got myself caught by Luther and I wasn't certain if I was going to live or die, you were there in my mind as strong as ever. And for that split second, when he had his gun aimed at me and I thought I was going to die, instead of fear, I felt a frustration so intense I wanted to yell. I didn't want to die without ever having held you . . . made love to you."

Her hands balled into fists as she fought the urge to move into his arms. Making love to her and allowing himself to be in love with her were not the same thing, she cautioned herself. The first was merely physical desire. She needed him to feel more than that. Silently she studied him, afraid to allow herself to hope he might be willing to let down the barrier he kept so securely around his heart.

He drew a terse breath as the hauntedness shadowed his features even more. "I decided you were right. It was time to allow Laura to accept at least some of the responsibility for her death. I've paid penance enough. After I left Doc's place this morning, I went by the cemetery and made my peace with myself and with her. I loved her. We shared a quiet comfortable love."

Samantha held her breath as he came closer and cupped her face in his hands. The sad haunted look in his eyes faded to be replaced by a warmth that caused her blood to race. "You, however, scare the hell out of me," he said. "You stir emotions in me that are so strong they unnerve me. You always have. I think that's why I worked so hard at keeping a distance between us even when we were young. I'm a man who likes to be in control and I never feel totally in control when you're around."

"Discovering how I really felt about you came as quite a shock to me," she reminded him.

Leaning down, he kissed her lightly. "I love you, Samantha. I figure being married to you won't be a smooth road, but it should be an interesting one. Marry me," he ordered.

Tears of joy welled in her eyes. He'd said he loved her! "I've always believed in obeying the law," she replied with a happy laugh, rising on tiptoe to kiss him back.

With a low growl of satisfaction, he drew her into his arms.

A little less than a month later, Samantha stood in the kitchen of Thatcher's home. It was early morning and she was starting a pot of coffee. The sun glinted on the gold band on her finger and she smiled. She was now Mrs. Thatcher Brant, and this wasn't Thatcher's home, it was *their* home.

Leona had been relieved to give up her job as housekeeper. "I'd forgotten how much energy it takes to look after two young children," the woman had said. She'd stayed on with Thatcher until his and Samantha's wedding, but now she was working for Jack Faraday at the drugstore and enjoying herself immensely. Samantha and Thatcher, and Maude and Howard had gotten married in a double ceremony. Samantha's parents had still seemed to be in a slight state of shock on the day of the wedding. A lot of people were, Samantha thought with a grin.

Madaline and Colin Darnell had even come back to Smytheshire for the ceremony. "I need to see this to believe it," Madaline had said when she'd heard of their plans to wed.

Even as Samantha was putting on her wedding gown, her sister, Joan, had asked her again if she knew what she was doing. When she'd assured Joan she knew exactly what she was doing, Joan had shaken her head and said, "Thatcher Brant and you as husband and wife is going to take some getting used to."

Walking down the aisle, Samantha had seen the dubious looks on the faces of several of their guests. But she'd never felt a moment of doubt herself.

"And I was right," she said with a soft smile, recalling how delicious waking in Thatcher's arms that morning had felt.

"Right about what?"

Samantha turned to see her husband entering the kitchen. "About marrying you. People said it wouldn't last. But we've made it through a whole week together."

Laughing, he approached and drew her into his arms. "Mom and Howard will be back in another week, then it's our turn. Johnny and Melissa are both looking forward to going and staying with them. I've got Charlie Norris lined up as a temporary deputy to help Dan, and you and I get to spend some time totally alone."

Samantha breathed an exaggerated sigh. "Just me and Thatcher Brant. I remember when people didn't think it was safe to leave us alone in the same room together."

"It still isn't," he growled, nipping her earlobe gently.

A fire ignited within her as his hands moved possessively along the lines of her body. "Not safe at all," she agreed.

Epilogue

Samantha stood at the window in the living room watching Thatcher leave for work. They'd been married for nearly six months now. On the table in front of her, among the plants and the framed pictures of them and other family members, sat her crystal sphere. Thatcher hadn't objected to her bringing it into his home. In fact, he'd insisted that she do just that. "It's been in your family for generations. It's a part of who you are," he'd said, as he'd placed it on the table in plain view.

And during the past months, he'd even shown an interest in it. Discretely, of course. However, his actions had caused some very surprising thoughts to begin playing around in her mind. She recalled the first time she and Thatcher had looked into the crystal together. The images had been sharper than they'd ever been before. She also remembered the look of concentration on his face and his admission he'd seen her reflection in the sphere. She'd never known the crystal to show reflections before or since. She'd attributed his irritation that night to the fact that he was angry with himself for even having gone to look at something he considered utter nonsense. Now she wasn't so sure that explanation was the correct one.

And, there was Mrs. Elberly's crystals. According to the elderly woman, they had an amazingly strong reaction to Thatcher. That, of course, didn't surprise her. Thatcher's presence had always rattled her. Still....

Samantha's mouth formed a thoughtful pout as she watched her husband driving away. It was very likely that he was alive today because she'd seen Luther in the sphere and gone to Mary's house to investigate. Maybe his changed attitude toward the crystal was because, although he'd never admitted it aloud, he knew he owed his life to it.

Or was his interest sparked by something more, she wondered. Was it possible that Thatcher also saw images in the crystal?

* * * * *

S SPRING FANCY

Three bachelors, footloose and fancy-free... until now!

Spring into romance with three fabulous fancies by three of Silhouette's hottest authors:

ANNETTE BROADRICK
LASS SMALL
KASEY MICHAELS

When spring fancy strikes, no man is immune!

Look for this exciting new short-story collection in March at your favorite retail outlet.

Only from

Silhouette®

SF93

where passion lives.

HE'S MORE THAN A MAN, HE'S ONE OF OUR

Fabulous Fathers

DAD GALAHAD
by Suzanne Carey

Confirmed bachelor Ned Balfour hadn't thought of himself as a knight in shining armor—until he met Jenny McClain. The damsel in distress had turned to Ned for help, and his sense of duty wouldn't let him disappoint the fair maiden. Jenny's baby needed a father and he vowed to become that man, even though mother and child would surely disrupt his solitary life. Could this ready-made family be the answer to Ned's quest for happiness?

Find out who does the true rescuing in Suzanne Carey's DAD GALAHAD. Available in April—only from Silhouette Romance!

Fall in love with our FABULOUS FATHERS—and join the Silhouette Romance family!

Silhouette
R O M A N C E™

FF493

Take 4 bestselling love stories FREE

Plus get a FREE surprise gift!

SMYTHESHIRE,
MASSACHUSETTS.

Small town. Big secrets.

Silhouette Romance invites you to visit Elizabeth August's intriguing small town, a place with an unusual legacy rooted deep in the past....

THE VIRGIN WIFE (#921) February 1993
HAUNTED HUSBAND (#922) March 1993
LUCKY PENNY (#945) June 1993
A WEDDING FOR EMILY (#953) August 1993

Elizabeth August's SMYTHESHIRE, MASSACHUSETTS—
This sleepy little town has plenty to keep you up at night.
Only from Silhouette Romance!

INTIMATE MOMENTS®
10TH
Anniversary

Celebrate our anniversary with a fabulous collection of firsts....

The first Intimate Moments titles written by three of your favorite authors:

NIGHT MOVES   Heather Graham Pozzessere
LADY OF THE NIGHT   Emilie Richards
A STRANGER'S SMILE   Kathleen Korbel

Silhouette Intimate Moments is proud to present a FREE hardbound collection of our authors' firsts—titles that you will treasure in the years to come from some of the line's founding members.

This collection will not be sold in retail stores and is available only through this exclusive offer. Look for details in Silhouette Intimate Moments titles available in retail stores in May, June and July.

Silhouette
ROMANCE™

COMING NEXT MONTH